J w a
3/14/82

NEVER BEFORE HAD A WOMAN
SPOKEN TO HIM
SO OPENLY OF HER NEEDS.

Longarm reached out, took Annabelle gently in his arms and drew her toward him. It was completely dark now, and the campfire had been reduced to glowing ashes. By its rosy light, he watched her step out of her dress.

Soon he was naked and she was settling beside him, desire leaping up from his loins as his kiss became urgent, angry almost. Then he moved swiftly over her so that she lay on the ground beneath him.

"Yes, Longarm!" she told him happily. "Oh, yes! I'm ready."

Also in the LONGARM series
from Jove

LONGARM
LONGARM ON THE BORDER
LONGARM AND THE AVENGING ANGELS
LONGARM AND THE WENDIGO
LONGARM IN THE INDIAN NATION
LONGARM AND THE LOGGERS
LONGARM AND THE HIGHGRADERS
LONGARM AND THE NESTERS
LONGARM AND THE HATCHET MEN
LONGARM AND THE MOLLY MAGUIRES
LONGARM AND THE TEXAS RANGERS
LONGARM IN LINCOLN COUNTY
LONGARM IN THE SAND HILLS
LONGARM IN LEADVILLE
LONGARM ON THE DEVIL'S TRAIL
LONGARM AND THE MOUNTIES
LONGARM AND THE BANDIT QUEEN
LONGARM ON THE YELLOWSTONE
LONGARM IN THE FOUR CORNERS
LONGARM AT ROBBER'S ROOST
LONGARM AND THE SHEEPHERDERS
LONGARM AND THE GHOST DANCERS
LONGARM AND THE TOWN TAMER
LONGARM AND THE RAILROADERS
LONGARM ON THE OLD MISSION TRAIL
LONGARM AND THE DRAGON HUNTERS
LONGARM AND THE RURALES
LONGARM ON THE HUMBOLDT
LONGARM ON THE BIG MUDDY
LONGARM SOUTH OF THE GILA
LONGARM IN NORTHFIELD
LONGARM AND THE GOLDEN LADY
LONGARM AND THE LAREDO LOOP
LONGARM AND THE BOOT HILLERS
LONGARM AND THE BLUE NORTHER
LONGARM ON THE SANTA FE
LONGARM AND THE STALKING CORPSE
LONGARM AND THE COMANCHEROS
LONGARM AND THE DEVIL'S RAILROAD
LONGARM IN SILVER CITY
LONGARM ON THE BARBARY COAST

TABOR EVANS

LONGARM

AND THE MOONSHINERS

A JOVE BOOK

LONGARM AND THE MOONSHINERS

Chapter 1

Longarm blinked unhappily at the woman standing at the foot of his bed. She was dressed entirely in black. Her raven hair was swept back into a tight bun, and the only color on her severe mourning dress was the gleaming gold necklace from which hung a gold cross. The woman was in her late thirties, handsome, with eyes that glowed with the fierce passion of those who seek to right old wrongs.

But it wasn't the cross or the woman's blazing eyes that made Longarm so melancholy this early in the morning. It was the Colt Peacemaker in her hands—in both her hands, actually, so heavy was the weapon. She was holding it out well in front of her, the cavernous muzzle yawning at Longarm like the entrance to Hades.

"Nice to see you, ma'am. Kind of early in the morning to visit a man in his bedroom, ain't it?"

"Yes," she said, and took a deep breath as she visibly steadied herself.

"Might be easier for both of us," Longarm suggested, slowly pushing himself to a sitting position, "if you'd tell me who you are."

"I am the daughter of Diego Sanchez, the man you brought in last night. The man you killed."

"Pleased to meet with you, Miss Sanchez. Would you mind pointing that cannon somewhere else?"

"I am going to kill you."

"You got the wrong man, ma'am. I didn't bring in any Diego Sanchez last night. I don't even know the gent."

"You lie. You do not wish for me to shoot you."

"Right on one, wrong on the other. I do not want you to shoot me, and I am not lying. How could I lie to a woman as beautiful as you?"

A flicker of uncertainty showed in the woman's dark eyes. "You are not this Longman?"

"That's right, ma'am. That's purely right. I am Alphonse Delight, a French drummer. I sell perfumes."

The gun wavered in her hands. "You do not look like a French seller of perfume."

"You do not look like a woman who would kill an innocent man."

The gun dropped an inch or so lower. She frowned in sudden confusion. "But is this not the right room?"

"No, it's not, ma'am. If you're looking for that there deputy U.S. marshal who works for the government, he's down the hall, first door on your right. Now if you'd just leave without slamming the door, I'd appreciate it. I'd like to get back to sleep. I've got a lot of customers to see tomorrow."

"You French," she said coldly, contemptuously, "you are strange people. You have no heart."

"I can't help what I am, ma'am, any more than you can."

She turned about swiftly, the skirts of her long black dress rustling as she hurried toward the door. Longarm watched her open it. She glanced back at him. He waved idly, then scrunched down as if to go back to sleep. She let herself out, closing the door after her slowly, firmly— without slamming it, precisely as Longarm had requested. It was obvious that Miss Sanchez was not an old hand at wreaking vengeance.

Longarm reached under his pillow for the polished walnut

grips of his double-action .44, slipped from the bed, and glided like a big cat across the room. Opening the door cautiously, he poked his head out and saw the woman in black letting herself into the room down the hall, the French perfume drummer's room.

Stepping out into the hallway, he cleared his throat. Loudly. The woman spun, saw him in the light from the wall lamp, and gasped. She knew in that instant that she had been tricked. He saw her swing up that big Colt she was carrying.

"Drop it, ma'am!" Longarm ordered.

But the woman wasn't listening. Longarm aimed quickly and fired at the wall about two feet over her head. The thunderous detonation—caught in the narrow confines of the hallway—caused his ears to ring. The awesome blast had a very discouraging effect on the woman also, especially when the plaster above her shining black hair showered down upon her.

She screamed as Longarm raised his Colt a second time, dropped her own weapon, and ran down the corridor, ducking out of sight at the next corner. Longarm ran on bare feet after her, and by the time he got to the stairwell, the French drummer and Mel White, the teamster, were charging into the hallway to investigate the fuss. Longarm pushed his way past the perfume salesman and rushed down the stairs. The door leading from the boardinghouse was closing behind Miss Sanchez when Longarm's landlady, wrapped in a comforter, poked her head out of her parlor.

To say she was shocked at the sight of Longarm's scantily clad frame would be an understatement. Her startled cry was enough to stop Longarm in his tracks. He glanced at the landlady, then back at the closed door leading to the street. With a weary shrug, he turned and hurried back up the stairs. Ignoring the teamster and the Frenchman, he picked up the weapon the woman had dropped on the hallway floor. Then he moved back into his room, slammed the door shut, and slumped down on his bed, both guns in his hands. Shuddering slightly at the memory of that crazed woman standing at the foot of his bed, he dropped his .44

3

onto the bed beside him and examined the woman's revolver.

It wasn't well kept, and the firing pin looked pretty well gummed up. Emptying the cylinder out onto the bed sheets, he discovered it contained only one round, and that one not under the firing pin.

There was a soft rap on his door.

"The door's open," Longarm said.

The teamster poked his head in. "You all right, Longarm?"

"I'm fine. Go back to sleep, Mel."

"I'll try, but that damned Frenchy is cursin' up a storm in his room next to mine."

"What's eating at him?"

"He says the first time he meets a woman eager to spend a night with him, you have to start shootin' at her. He's plumb put out, he is."

"Tell him to go back to sleep. If she'd gone all the way into his room, she would have killed him. I saved his life."

"That the truth, Longarm?"

Longarm sighed. "Likely not, judging from this weapon. But just tell him what I said, Mel."

"Sure, Longarm."

As the teamster hastily closed the door and padded down the hall to the drummer's room, Longarm shook his head wearily and looked out the window. It was almost light. Through the open window, that familiar, unmistakable odor of burning leaves wafted into the room. Mingling with it and threatening to overpower it were the stronger and not nearly so pleasant smells of coal smoke and horse manure. The steady clop of a milkman's horse echoed in the narrow street below his window. Somewhere a dog barked. Longarm sighed. He was wide awake, every sense alert. It would do him no good to try to get back to sleep, not now, not even if he dared.

With a weary shrug, he got to his feet and padded over to his dresser. Staring back at him from the tarnished mirror was the lean, lived-in face that belonged to a man on the comfortable side of forty. An unblinking sun and unforgiving winds had cured his rawboned features to a saddle-leather brown. He might have been mistaken for an Indian if it had not been for the gunmetal blue of his wide-set eyes, the tobacco-leaf color of his hair and uptwisted longhorn mustache, and the dark stubble on his lantern jaw.

A train entered the Union Yards a quarter-mile away and let loose with a long, quavering whistle. Reaching for the bottle of Maryland rye on the dresser, Longarm took a healthy swig to settle himself down some, then set to work making himself presentable for the coming day.

Stripping off his long johns, he used the last of his Maryland rye and the water from the pitcher on his dresser for a cold whore's-bath, then stepped back into his underwear. Plucking his gray cotton-flannel shirt from where it hung on a bedpost, he buttoned it and reached for the brown tweed trousers hanging on the other bedpost. He pulled the britches on and cursed the fly shut; the pants fit like a second skin around his upper thighs and hips, a practical necessity for a man whose travels occasionally took him into brushy country, and whose job was such that a pair of pants caught on a bramble at the wrong moment might make a mortal difference.

He sighed and shook his head as he picked up a black string tie from the dresser top and knotted it under his shirt collar. Some bureaucrat back in Washington had decided that federal employees like Longarm had to wear these nooses around their necks while on duty, though Longarm usually shed the fool thing once he was out of sight of the home office.

Bending double, he pulled on a pair of woolen socks, then grunted his feet into his cordovan cavalry stovepipes. They were low-heeled and as tight as his pants because, as a working lawman, he spent as much time afoot as he did astride a horse, and he could run with surprising speed for a man his size in boots that fit as tightly as these did—a fact that many an unhorsed outlaw had learned to his dismay as he hobbled frantically over the landscape in high-heeled riding boots with Longarm in pursuit.

Longarm slipped the supple leather belt of his cross-draw

rig around his waist, adjusting it to ride just above his hipbones. He put on a vest that matched his pants, swept his change off the top of his dresser, and dropped the money into his pants pocket. Then he picked up his wallet. He had only a single twenty-dollar silver certificate in it—not nearly enough to last him till payday, unless he got lucky at poker at the Windsor. His silver federal badge was pinned inside the wallet. He rubbed it once on his shirtsleeve, then folded the wallet, slipped on his dark brown frock coat, and tucked the wallet away in an inside pocket.

A handful of extra cartridges and a bundle of waterproof kitchen matches were in the right side pocket of his coat. The left-hand pocket held his pair of handcuffs. The key to the cuffs and his room joined a jackknife in his left pants pocket.

Then, with some care, Longarm lifted the Ingersoll watch from the top of his dresser. Attached to the watch was a long, gold-washed chain. Clipped to the other end of the chain was the brass butt of a double-barreled .44 derringer. The watch rode in the vest's left breast pocket, the derringer in the matching pocket on the right, the chain looping across Longarm's nearly flat vest front between them.

Ready now for the world—and any more irate daughters in black vowing vengeance—Longarm tucked a clean linen handkerchief into the breast pocket of his frock coat, then lifted his snuff-brown Stetson from its peg on the wall. He positioned it dead center on his head, tilted slightly forward, cavalry style—the crown telescoped in the Colorado rider's fashion—and left his room.

Cautiously.

The dim hallway ahead of him was apparently empty, so he moved—or rather, *loomed*—through the semidarkness to the stairs and glided swiftly down them and out into Denver's chill early-morning light. He was too early by at least two hours to report to Marshal Billy Vail's office, but he knew an all-night greasy spoon off Colfax where the coffee was strong enough to jolt him fully awake, and the rest of the breakfast would be hearty enough to set him up for a day or two.

As he headed up the cinder path to the Colfax Avenue

bridge, the smell of burning leaves seemed to grow more pungent with each step he took.

Chief Marshal Billy Vail pulled himself to a startled halt when he saw Longarm waiting for him on the steps of the Federal Building. He clawed for his pocket watch, studied its face in some wonderment, then pocketed it and continued toward his deputy.

"Didn't mean to give you a stroke, Billy," Longarm drawled, as the still-astonished marshal pulled up in front of him.

Vail screwed his face into a frown. A man who in his salad days had ridden many an outlaw's ass into the ground, the marshal had long since gone to lard, wrestling with the paper blizzard that drifted in from Washington. His sagging jowls and belly were a constant reminder to Longarm that he should stay away from pastry and insist on long, hard-riding jobs that would take him safely away from the soft enticements of this city. The last thing Longarm wanted was to end his days in Marshal Vail's physical condition. But he liked Vail and respected him. The aging lawman had forgotten more about tracking and living off the country than Longarm could ever hope to learn.

"What is it, Longarm? How come you're out here so early? Christ, even the pigeons haven't shown up yet."

"A woman in black woke me up very early this morning, Billy."

"Hell, that should've made you *late*," Vail said, a smile creasing the older lawman's soft face. "What's the matter? Losin' your touch?"

"This old girl had a very big Colt in her hand, and she was pointing it at my head. She said she was Diego's daughter."

"Might be. He had one, sure enough. She lived with him at Rose Fork until he lit out to rob that stage."

"She's after me because I brought Diego in dead."

"Don't really blame her, at that."

"I told you how that happened. He got loose and came at me with a case knife. I didn't shoot to kill, just to cripple him up some, but the poor son of a bitch lost his footing."

7

"And you blew his head off instead. Yeah. I read your report before I left the office last night. I ain't faultin' you, Longarm. Just one of them things. But I can see this girl's unhappiness. What happened? You didn't have to rough her up, did you?"

"I scared her and she lit out. Turned out the weapon she was using wasn't all that deadly."

"So what do you want me to do?"

"Find her and talk some sense into her. The next time she might get lucky."

"I'll put Wallace on it."

"Fine. Meanwhile, get me out of town. I don't want to tangle with her again. I already killed her old man. I don't want to add any more woe to that family."

Vail shrugged. "As far as I know, that's all the family that's left."

Longarm sagged; that fact did not make him feel any better.

Vail tipped his bald head and looked up at Longarm. "I was going to send Wallace out on a job I was sure you wouldn't want to take—but maybe now you'll be more reasonable."

"Where is it?"

"Come on. I'll tell you inside."

As Billy Vail led the way into the courthouse, Longarm glanced quickly down the street up which the marshal had just walked. For a split second he thought he saw a woman in black. But when he looked again, he saw nothing. Ashamed at himself for acting like a spooked colt, he followed Vail into the building. He didn't care what Billy Vail had for him, as long as it got him out of Denver. He didn't like waking up with the muzzle of a sixgun inches from his face, no matter what its condition.

Longarm shifted unhappily in the chief's red leather armchair and began to chew on his unlit cheroot. "Since when," he said, "are we interested in a few enterprising grangers who decide to manufacture a little moonshine on the side? I had an uncle who paid his taxes and stood by the Union,

8

but he sure as hell made the best white lightning this side of paradise. That's an art, Billy, not a crime. Besides, we work for Justice, not Treasury. Let them bag their own moonshiners."

"Now just hold on there a minute, Longarm. I know how you feel about moonshiners, and I happen to agree with you. But in this case we've got a mix that's not what it should be—and that maybe puts it in our laps, after all."

"What kind of a mix?"

"Murder, Longarm. Murder. Bodies mutilated, and some talk that the Shoshone done it."

"Talk? Is that all?"

"That's all, but that's enough. Your old friend Colonel Walthers is just itchin' to move on them Shoshone, and the Bureau of Indian Affairs is pissin' in its collective pants at the thought. The last thing we need is another Indian uprising."

"You sure got my head spinning, Billy. What's Shoshones got to do with moonshining?"

"Damn it, listen. It's got my head spinning too. Them mutilated bodies belongs to revenue agents, U.S. Government employees. Four of them by last count, and two more probably on the way, since they ain't been heard from for a couple of weeks. There's no way we can look the other way, Longarm, and call this just a Treasury matter."

"You say the agents' bodies were mutilated."

"Yes."

"How?"

"Jesus, Longarm. You want the details, do you?"

"I sure as hell do."

"Why, damn it?"

"Never mind that, Billy. Just tell me what you've got there."

The marshal sighed, pawed through the pile of papers on his desk, and eventually pulled out the folder he was looking for. As he opened it, Longarm lit his cheroot and leaned back, his eyes attentive through the swirling smoke.

"Well now," Billy Vail began, "it looks like the usual. Scalps taken, fingers cut off, stuff like that." Vail looked up at Longarm. "Is that enough detail for you?"

"Not hardly, but it'll do for starters. Does it say how large the scalps were?"

"How *large?*"

"That's right. How much of the scalp was missing," Longarm explained patiently.

Vail glanced back down at the file. Frowning, he said, "The whole damn top of their heads was taken, looks like. One fellow was described as having his scalp just about peeled off his head."

"The Shoshone ain't killing them revenue men, Billy," Longarm said quietly. "The Cheyenne are the only ones who cut off the fingers of their dead enemies. And they take sizable scalps. The Shoshone take small scalps once in a while, but not too often. Looks like someone familiar with Cheyenne ways is trying to frame the Shoshones. Either that or it's Cheyenne, not Shoshone, behind these killings."

"I doubt that, Longarm."

"Me too, Billy."

"Find out what the hell's going on up there, Longarm," Vail said, handing the folder to him. "Look this over carefully. If them moonshiners are killing Treasury men and trying to blame it on the Shoshone, we want *their* scalps."

"That's Snake River country?" Longarm asked, taking the folder.

"That's right."

"Where'd they find the bodies?"

"A little place called Taylor's Ferry, due north of Ogden, Utah. The last they heard of them revenue agents was in Red Gap, northwest of Taylor's Ferry, near the Beaverheads. You know the country, don't you?"

"How much help can I count on from the locals?"

"Damn little. They've got their hands full just keeping alive up there, without bothering to traipse into the mountains after moonshiners, who're more than likely their own people."

"So that leaves a clear field for that idiot, Colonel Walthers."

"Precisely, Longarm. Now I can *still* send Wallace if you'd rather. Just give him that folder when he gets in."

10

"Never mind about that. I'll leave Wallace here to handle that Sanchez woman."

"You want us to throw the book at her when he finds her?"

"No. Just wise her up. Tell her how it was. Tell her I didn't mean to kill her father. I had no choice."

"You think she'll believe us?"

"No, but it might slow her down some. In time, she should cool off."

Vail nodded. "Makes sense, I suppose."

Longarm stood up, dropping his cheroot into the spittoon next to Billy Vail's desk. "I'm low on funds, Billy. I'll need some travel money and a train ticket to Ogden."

"See my clerk when he gets in. Meanwhile, study that folder."

A glance at the banjo clock on the wall told Longarm it was not yet eight o'clock. He decided he'd go outside and wait for the clerk to show up, just to see the look of surprise on the young man's face when he walked in and saw Longarm there ahead of him for once.

The ride from Taylor's Ferry to Red Gap took Longarm three days. He found the settlement at the end of a steep-walled valley, huddled on a bench close under a titanic wall of rock that seemed to reach almost straight up, dwarfing the bench and the town sitting upon it. As he followed the trail through the valley toward the toylike settlement in the distance, nearly perpendicular walls of rock sloped sharply skyward on both sides of him. The giant firs that somehow clung to the sheer walls appeared as tiny and insubstantial as twigs.

It was almost sundown by the time he had ridden close enough to pick out the individual buildings that made up the town of Red Gap. Below the town ran a swift mountain stream, over which a crude plank bridge had been thrown. A moment later he was clopping across the bridge into Red Gap.

He was not impressed by what the light of a dying day revealed to him. None of the frame buildings had seen a paintbrush or were likely to in the future, and nearly every

11

structure's sagging ridgepoles and weathered, warped walls
bore mute testimony to the mean winters that were common
this high up on the Continental Divide. The streets that ran
between the buildings were little more than muddy, rutted
trails. There was the usual cluster of businesses along what
appeared to be the main street: blacksmith shop, barbershop,
funeral parlor, saloon, general store, and post office. The
only hotel in the town was a three-story affair, by far the
most imposing building in Red Gap.

Riding past the single saloon, Longarm saw its sagging
porch suddenly blossom with poorly shaven, overfed hard-
cases who drifted out to take a long, cold look at this newcomer riding into their midst. Longarm understood perfectly
the hostility he read in their faces. Until Longarm was able
to prove differently, these men would have no choice but
to consider him another Treasury agent come to flush out
local moonshiners. Riding on past the saloon, he nudged
his mount over to the hitch rail in front of the hotel and
dismounted.

The hotel's lobby doubled as the town post office, and
as Longarm entered it, a surprisingly pretty woman in her
late thirties left the small cubicle that served as the post
office, and paused behind the front desk. She smiled pleas-
antly as Longarm reached her.

"Room for one, sir?"

"That's right, ma'am."

"You have plenty to choose from. You're the first guest
I've had in weeks, almost."

"Almost?"

She smiled. "Two guests that checked in a few weeks
ago just up and disappeared. I can't understand it. My cooking couldn't be that bad." She handed him a pen and turned
the register so he could sign it.

"I'm sure it isn't, ma'am," he said, signing the register.

Her smiled deepened. "Room four," she told him. "The
best room in the house." She turned the register and glanced
down at his name. "I hope you enjoy your stay in Red Gap,
Mr. Long."

Longarm smiled back at her. "I hope I don't just up and

disappear, like those other gentlemen. Maybe you could describe them to me. When you've got the time, that is."

"Of course. I'd be delighted." She handed him the key to his room.

About two hours later, after Longarm had attended to his horse and eaten a hearty supper in the hotel's small dining room, he was settling himself back on his bed. The ride had been a grueling one, and his camps under the cold stars had not been an unmitigated joy. The soft life of Denver had taken more of a toll of his willingness to sleep on rocky beds than he had realized.

He stretched wearily, luxuriously, and was about to close his eyes when he heard a soft rap on his door. Coming alert at once, he unholstered his Colt. Carrying it lightly in his right hand, he left his bed and stole to one side of the door.

"Yes?"

"It's me. The postmistress."

Longarm opened the door. As the postmistress—a mischievous gleam in her eye—entered and saw the weapon in Longarm's hand, she laughed. "I won't hurt you, Mr. Long. I promise. You can put away your weapon."

"Just a precaution," Longarm said, closing the door and returning the Colt to its holster, which hung from the bedpost over his pillow.

"I see you're relaxing," she said.

Longarm nodded. He was wearing only his pants and socks. He had taken off his frock coat, vest, and shirt—even his hat, which he had placed on the small dresser near the window.

"Perhaps I shouldn't disturb you."

"I rode a long ways, ma'am," he said. "From Taylor's Landing."

"Yes, that must have been very wearying. If you wish, I can return later."

"What was it you wanted, ma'am?"

"You asked me to give you descriptions of those two men who disappeared. I said I would, when I had the time. Well, the post office is closed now, and I don't expect any

13

more weary travelers from Boise at this hour, so here I am."

"Well, that's right helpful, ma'am."

"My name is Marge. Marge Pennock. I own this hotel, and the federal government has rewarded my industry and enterprise by making me the postmistress in this town."

"You are a woman of substance."

"Yes," she said carefully. "In Red Gap, I am."

"There's only one chair. If you'd sit there, Marge, I'll sit back down on the bed."

She sat. Longarm sat also, and took a long look at his guest. There was not a weak line in Marge Pennock's face, which was square, open, and handsome. A dimple in the middle of her chin and her sensitive, delicate brows erased any possible masculine overtones. Her green eyes were dazzling, especially when she smiled. There was nothing slight or girlish about her figure. It was ripe without being obtrusive, and the long, dark blue, wasp-waisted dress she wore only seemed to enhance her body's mature swell. Longarm got the impression that she was a woman who knew exactly how to use—and enjoy—her body.

He also got the impression that she might very well have run other kinds of houses in the past.

"Well, do you like what you see?" Marge asked, smiling.

"No complaints, Marge."

"That's fine. Because I like what I see, too."

"You say you could give me a description of those two men?"

"A description and their names." She appraised him coolly. "You're a lawman, are you not?"

"Deputy U.S. Marshal Custis Long, at your service, ma'am."

"I thought so. Well, their names were Dick Wilson and Tom Moon. They had 'revenue agent' written all over them, and they asked a lot of questions, then hired some horses from the livery and rode out of town."

"Didn't they ride in on their own mounts?"

"Yes, what was left of them. They rode those poor critters right into the ground. They were lousy horsemen, I'd say."

"And neither man has been heard of since?"

"That's correct."

14

"How long have they been gone?"

"It will be two weeks tomorrow."

"Describe them to me, Marge."

"Wilson was a tall beanpole; his partner was not as tall, but twice as big. Moon had no hair under his derby, and Wilson had a loose, straggly thatch of red hair. Neither man wore a mustache, and they were dressed a lot like you, but not as neat."

"Thank you."

"You're welcome."

Longarm knew those two men had been sent up here. It had been in the folder Vail had given him to study. Wilson and Moon. And Marge was right, of course. They were Treasury agents, on the trail of moonshiners.

Longarm got to his feet. "Thank you very much, Marge. I hope I can return the favor sometime. I'll need all the cooperation I can get in this town, I am sure."

She smiled and got to her feet also. "You can thank me right now, Mr. Long," she said, walking up to him and flinging her arms around his neck.

Her kiss was bold and provocative. He felt her hands moving down his back and then thrusting down into his waistband. Clasping his buttocks, she thrust him hard against her and began to move seductively. Her lips still fastened to his, she forced him gently backward until the backs of his knees struck the edge of the bed.

He fell back with Marge still on him. He tried to help her with his britches, but she slapped his hands away, kept on kissing him, and skinned him—swiftly and expertly. By that time he had managed to unbutton the back of her dress and peel it back. As he had surmised the moment she had thrust her body against his, she wore nothing under her dress. They rolled over on the bed, still clasped in each other's arms, lips and tongues still entwined.

"Ma'am," Longarm gasped, "I purely wish you'd wait a minute—give me a chance to get into a proper position."

"Nonsense," she said, scooting under him and thrusting upward. "No need for that." She fastened her lips back onto his.

Longarm found himself inside Marge Pennock, plunging

15

incredibly deep as her legs swung up and scissored themselves securely about his back.

It wasn't long before Longarm discovered what it was like to be raped—and he wasn't entirely sure he liked it. He figured he would have to try it a few more times to find out for sure.

Chapter 2

Longarm's breakfast the next morning was a feast to remember. As if she were stoking a fire that she was afraid
would go out, the postmistress took care of the preparation
of Longarm's breakfast herself, banging happily about in
the kitchen with an occasional song on her lips.

After starting him off with a dish of hot biscuits, she
placed before him an enormous platter of fried eggs, home
fries, bacon, sausage, and thick slabs of homemade bread,
topped off with generous squares of fresh butter, and a huge
jar of marmalade. The coffee that finished the meal was as
pungent and satisfying as any he had ever made for himself
on the trail.

At the end of the meal, the postmistress joined him in
a cup of coffee, obviously enjoying the relish with which
Longarm put away her vittles. At last, finishing his third
cup of coffee, Longarm put his empty cup down into its
saucer, patted his stomach contentedly, and pushed himself
carefully away from the table. "You set a fine table,
ma'am," he told her.

She smiled at his compliment. There was a faint smudge

of flour on the tip of her nose. "Always liked to cook for a man knows how to eat," she said. "As long as he knows how to do other things as well." She smiled wickedly. "I trust you slept well last night?"

"Like a rock. You plumb tuckered me out, ma'am."

"I slept well myself," she admitted, a blush resting momentarily on her cheeks.

There was a loud yell from the lobby. Both of them looked in that direction. Standing in the dining room doorway was a powerful-looking man in his early forties. He had shoulders to match a grizzly's, and arms like telegraph poles. His beard hid everything but his cheekbones, nose, and eyes. It looked like he was peering at them both from out of an impenetrable bush. He was wearing a black floppy-brimmed hat pulled down low over his forehead, and had wrapped himself from head to foot in various scarfs and blankets. A huge Navy Colt was stuck in the thick leather belt that held up his buckskin britches.

"Smitty!" Marge cried, jumping up. "When did you get in?"

"Just now, Marge. An' it looks like your mail sack is gettin' lighter with each trip."

"I don't wonder," said Marge, hurrying over to greet Smitty. "Who's going to write a letter to anyone dumb enough to spend their life in a place like this?"

She kissed Smitty on the tip of his nose and gave him a quick hug. The big man clapped her heartily on the back, then turned his attention to Longarm.

"An' who might this gent be?" he inquired.

Longarm had gotten to his feet by this time. He advanced on Smitty with his hand outstretched. "Name's Long," he told Smitty, shaking the big fellow's hand. Smitty's grip was a firm and powerful one. "Custis Long."

"Roland Smith," the fellow replied. "My friends call me Smitty."

"They better," said Marge, with a grin.

"*My* friends call me Longarm," Longarm replied.

"He's a deputy U.S. marshal," Marge told Smitty. "He's come to investigate the killings."

Smitty peered at Longarm shrewdly. "What killings?"

18

"Those four revenuers found mutilated near Taylor's Ferry," Longarm told him. "The men that were washed up along the shore. They were probably killed near here, then dumped into the Snake."

Smitty pinched his nose between his thumb and forefinger and gave it a slight twist. Then he rubbed it, his shrewd little eyes regarding Longarm carefully. "A dastardly deed, that," Smitty agreed, nodding his massive head emphatically. "And it don't look like we seen the last of it, neither. A couple more revenuers done disappeared from here a while back." He looked speculatively at Longarm. "They just sent you in, did they? All by your lonesome?"

"That's right. Just me."

"That don't seem hardly sensible. No, it don't. At the rate them revenuers been dumped—all cut up like you said they was—I was thinkin' the government would send in the army, or a posse, at least."

"Especially since it might be Indians," said Marge.

"Don't see why we have to jump to that conclusion," Longarm said.

Smitty looked warily at Longarm. "Seems to me I been hearing that maybe some renegade Shoshone might be responsible. You know something I don't, maybe?"

"Nope."

"Usually," said Marge, "such a number of killing's would go big in the eastern papers. I was wondering, when you first came in last night, if maybe you were that fellow Buntline—or a New York reporter."

"Sorry, Marge," Longarm told her with a smile. "I'm just a lone deputy from Denver."

"You came all that way, huh?" said Smitty. "Well, I guess that shows somethin'." He paused a moment, sizing Longarm up. "Good luck, Deputy. You got your work cut out for you. Them moonshiners—or whoever is killin' them revenuers—is a law unto themselves. Yes, they is. I'd rather be back trappin' beaver and fightin' the Cheyenne than packin' this here mail through their country. They figure any stranger is an enemy."

"But they know you now," said Marge, patting Smitty's huge arm. "They wouldn't shoot you, Smitty."

The big man grinned. He did not have all of his teeth, and those he had were yellowed stumps. "Not unless they took a mind to, they wouldn't. But they know they'd better kill me first thing, or I'd track them to hell and gone. They knows that for sure."

Marge looked at Longarm, her head resting on Smitty's huge shoulder. "You see why Smitty is the only one I can trust to pack in the mail?" she asked him. "I don't know what this town would do without him."

"I didn't have much trouble riding in," Longarm said.

"That's right. You didn't," agreed Smitty with another toothless grin. "But you ain't tried to ride *out* yet."

"Where might I find these moonshiners?"

"Just ride back out that valley you rode through on your way into Red Gap, and when you get to the other side, go north through the pass. You'll find yourself in high country with parks aplenty, filled with game, and good rich farmland along the river when you get over the second ridge. Never saw such a pretty land. Just keep ridin'. Them moonshiners'll find you soon enough."

"What are their names?"

"There's two families that lords it over the rest—the MacLaggans and the Radleys. Dennis MacLaggan is the leader, a fine broth of a man, he is—and a man who knows how to capture pure lightnin' in a bottle. It's a shame such a gift be a crime. A real shame."

"I'm not a revenue officer, Smitty. I just want whoever is behind the killing of those Treasury men. I'm after murderers, not moonshiners."

"You'd better make that plain right off, then," said Smitty.

"Yes," agreed Marge. "Right off. That Simpson Radley has a fierce temper. He ain't the gentleman MacLaggan is."

"Come on, Marge," said Smitty, looking down at the woman. "I was seen ridin' in. You'd better get after that no-account clerk of yours to help you sort the mail. There'll be a crowd out there soon enough, I'm thinkin'."

Marge nodded in agreement, winked goodbye to Longarm, and hurried out of the dining room toward the large sacks of mail Smitty had dumped before the front desk.

20

Smitty looked at Longarm. "Care to join me in a snifter, Deputy? It's been a long, dry ride for me and my men."

"Too early. I'll be riding out soon, and from what you just said, it'd be a good idea if I kept a clear head and a steady hand for them MacLaggans."

"You'll need both," Smitty agreed. "Count on it. But don't you dare turn down a drink if they offer. They'd call it a personal insult."

"Thanks, Smitty, I'll remember that."

Longarm returned to his room, picked up his gear, and walked across to the livery stable to saddle his horse. Mounting up, he ducked his head and cantered out through the big doorway onto the street. A large crowd was already clustered on the hotel porch, its members waiting not too patiently for their chance to crowd into the small hotel lobby for their mail. A long line of Smitty's packhorses, some of them still not relieved of their considerable burdens, was strung out along the narrow main street. Longarm counted twelve in all.

Smitty's men were not too diligent in unloading the animals, it appeared, despite the complaints of the merchants awaiting their merchandise. And Smitty, already feeling the effects of his early-morning liquid breakfast, was no help at all as he began passing bottles among his men. Longarm waved as he rode past Smitty on his way out of town. But the teamster was too busy to wave back. He was trying to free a merchant from one of his men, a one-eyed blackguard with a red bandanna wrapped about his skull.

Clopping over the wooden bridge a moment later, Longarm reflected on Red Gap's isolation. It was obvious that the merchants and other townspeople could not be very happy, having to depend entirely on Roland Smith's packhorses for supplies and mail. A town without a stage line or a railroad to serve it was a pretty sorry, lonely place, sure enough.

An hour later, Longarm found himself riding through the land Smitty had described to him. Rimmed by formidable ranks of sooty black rocks, the long, open valley was obviously filled with pockets of fairly rich soil, judging from

21

the lush abundance of grama and buffalo grass that carpeted the parks and open meadows.

The lower, wooded section of this high, open land was timbered for the most part with aspen groves, their trembling olive-green leaves gleaming in the sunlight. He kept himself well above the aspens whenever he could, however, since the streams that flowed through them were alive with beaver. They chewed hell out of the aspens and dammed almost any little rill, with the result that their dams backed the water into the timber, transforming the woodlands into soggy, cool jungles that were unpleasantly alive with ticks, as Longarm had discovered during his trip through the Yellowstone country a while back.

He kept going until he had put the aspens behind him, aware by this time that the ground was lifting gently but surely under him. The rimrocks he passed now were no longer so high above him, and their color did not appear to be as uniform as before. Some were thrusting fists, the color of a dun horse or a gray. Others were a rich, dark brown. Occasional outcroppings of basalt, like the hilts of Indian knives, were visible. In this thinner, poorer soil there were more rocks visible, and the clump and cheat grass were already beginning to crowd out the buffalo and grama. Scrub juniper, pine, and spruce began to dot the slopes. The smell of sage was carried on the cool, sometimes chill, breezes that swept down from the towering, snow-capped peaks that hung above him in the western sky.

He was afoot, watering his horse in an ice-cold spring that gushed from a small embankment, when he caught sight of some cattle grazing on a dry benchland just beyond the next ridge. They did not look good, even at the two hundred yards or so that separated them from Longarm. They were scrub and lean—sorry, unhappy specimens. He counted close to twenty head in all, then looked around more carefully in an attempt to see if there were any ranch houses or line shacks in the vicinity.

He saw no line shacks and no ranch houses. What he did see, however, was the gleam of sunlight on a rifle barrel.

It came from among the basalt rocks poking up along the rim of the valley. Longarm did not let his gaze pause, but kept his head moving. Then he looked back to his horse, pulling it gently away from the spring. Mounting up, he guided his mount down a long draw that took him to a flat bordering a heavy stand of spruce. He cantered toward the spruce, spooking a gaunt steer out of his path, then ducked his head and rode into the timber.

He kept going for at least a couple hundred yards before dismounting. Tying his mount to a sapling on the rim of a brook-fed patch of small meadow, he snaked his Winchester from his saddle, jumped across the brook, and moved still farther into the timber before cutting back toward the rimrocks.

He came out of the timber in a better position than he had hoped for—behind a towering bluff that shielded him from the rimrocks above. He moved swiftly up the steep, talus-littered slope until he reached a narrow game trail that paralleled the ridge above. He gained the ridge finally, then picked his way along it for close to half a mile before he reckoned he was within gunshot range of the bushwhacker he was searching for.

He pulled up cautiously and began to pick his way very slowly over the rocky terrain. The sound of a horse blowing almost directly in front of him—followed by the unmistakable clink of a horse's bit—caused Longarm to pull up suddenly. He waited a while longer, heard nothing more, then peered cautiously over a dark blade of rock that stood between him and the ridge beyond.

Standing in full view less than ten yards away was the rifleman he had glimpsed from below.

He was a tall, exceedingly lank fellow with wrists that hung at least six inches out of his sleeves, and britches that were cut so short the man's anklebones were as visible as his wrists. He had no stockings on, and the shoes he wore seemed at least a couple of sizes too large. His red plaid shirt had faded to a dull orange, and a torn, black floppy-brimmed hat sat well back on his narrow skull. The fellow looked to be in his early twenties, but something in the way he handled his gleaming, well-kept Winchester warned Longarm that he was no child in a man's country.

The man was still peering at the timber into which Longarm had vanished, but he was standing in full view now, making no effort to keep himself hidden. Abruptly he started talking to someone out of Longarm's field of vision—and to Longarm's surprise, the response came from someone who must have been standing just in front of Longarm, on the other side of the rock behind which he himself was hiding.

"There ain't no sense in waitin' any longer, Bob," this other one replied. From the sound of his voice, Longarm judged him to be a few years younger than the fellow standing on the ridge. "He'll come out on Rad's spread when he gets to the other side. Then Rad can deal with him."

"Rad'll kill him."

"No he won't, Tim. He'll put him to work first. *Then* he'll kill him."

"Like he killed them revenuers?"

"We ain't sure he done that."

"Someone did. And what about them other two agents that Rad's got now? He's usin' them like slaves. It don't seem natural to use men that way."

"That ain't none of our concern."

Longarm straightened and was about to step boldly out from behind the rock when he heard the soft chink of spurs behind him. Before he could turn, he felt the cold steel of a rifle barrel press gently against the back of his neck.

"Drop that rifle, mister," a deep, husky voice said.

Longarm did as he was told and turned to find himself looking at a man in his early forties. He was exceedingly fat. His eyes, small and unpleasant, peered at Longarm out of a raw, drooping face so red that it looked scalded. His nose was a bulbous, red-veined button, his mouth a dark, fanged sneer.

"Lookee what I got here, Bobby!" the fellow called.

The two others had heard the newcomer's order to Longarm to drop his rifle, and were already around the rock, approaching cautiously, their rifles at the ready.

"Christ, Lester," said Bobby. "I thought he rode on through the timber."

"I caught sight of him coming out of it north of here. It

24

weren't likely he was up to any good, so I followed him. Your daddy would not be pleased with the way you handled this here feller, Bob. This damn revenuer come near bushwhacking you both."

"I had no such intention," drawled Longarm.

"Shut up!" said Lester. "No one is speakin' to you!" As he spoke, Lester emphasized his words with a deep, cruel thrust into Longarm's stomach with the rifle barrel.

"And I'm not a Treasury agent," Longarm said, doing his best to ignore the thrust. "I'm a deputy U.S. marshal."

"Shit," said Lester. "Same difference. *Trouble* is what you are, mister. But we know how to take care of your likes—even if these here two MacLaggans don't."

"You takin' him?" the lanky MacLaggan asked, frowning suddenly.

"You bet I am," Lester replied. "I'm the one found him, ain't I? Besides, we needs help bringing in the rest of that barley."

Bob nodded, then looked at his brother, "Let's go, Tim."

But Tim did not budge. He was a clear-eyed youngster of eighteen or so, with light red hair and shockingly blue eyes. "I don't think it's right for you to do this, Lester," the young man said. "You're makin' slaves of these men, that's what you are. And maybe you're the one that's killin' them when you get through with them. You heard what this man said. He ain't no Treasury agent. He's a deputy U.S. marshal. You'll have the army in here next."

Lester grinned coldly at the young man. "I ought to cuff you for that impertinence," he said, "but you ain't dry yet behind the ears, Tim boy. So I'll just let it pass this time. Now you go back home and tell MacLaggan he better not send any more boys on a man's job the next time. You knew this feller was on the way. They ain't no excuse for not stoppin' him before he got into that timber."

"Come on, Tim," said Bob, taking his brother's arm and pulling him in the direction of a nearby clump of pine. "We better get back."

Tim hesitated a moment, then went reluctantly with his brother.

"Now then," said Lester to Longarm, as soon as the two had moved off, "let's see what kind of weapon you carry, mister."

Keeping the barrel of his rifle still thrust into Longarm's midsection, Lester leaned forward and flipped Longarm's frock coat open. When he saw the cross-draw rig and the walnut grips on the lawman's .44, he smiled in appreciation and lifted the Colt out of the holster. Hefting it expertly, he said, "Nice iron, this. I don't see as I'd have much use for that fancy a rig, though."

Lester stepped quickly back. His greedy little eyes had lit for a moment on Longarm's watch, but the man obviously did not think it wise to stay too close to the tall lawman for any length of time. Besides, he undoubtedly figured, he could always take Longarm's valuables later.

"You dress right fancy for a lawman, and that's a fact," Lester said, "but we'll take that polish off you soon enough. Do you good, it will. Never did see a government agent didn't have soft hands and a soft middle to go with 'em."

Tim and Bob MacLaggan rode out of the pines then. With a wave to Lester, they cut north toward a mass of rocks sitting on a farther ridge. In a moment they had disappeared beyond it.

"You left that horse of yours in the timber, did you?" Lester asked Longarm.

"That's right."

"So that means you walk. My horse's over here. Keep ahead of me and don't make no sudden moves."

For the next half hour or so, Longarm did as he was told. With his mounted captor riding just behind him, he retraced the path along the ridge he had taken earlier. When they came to the game trail, Lester dismounted and led his horse, keeping the barrel of his Winchester thrust into Longarm's back as they moved cautiously along the narrow trail. Later, the steep, talus-littered slope caused Lester some difficulty, since he had to lead his horse as well as keep Longarm under his control. Longarm did what he could to increase the man's problems by repeatedly losing his footing and having to scramble to stay upright. But it did no good. Lester was able to keep the muzzle of his rifle lodged firmly

26

in the small of Longarm's back.

Then, near the bottom of the slope, Longarm heard Lester swear furiously and felt the pressure of the rifle barrel in his back suddenly vanish. Glancing over his shoulder, Longarm saw Lester reaching around for his horse's reins. The terrified animal was rearing frantically in an effort to find solid footing in the treacherously shifting talus.

Longarm ducked his head and let himself slip, then tumble head over heels down the slope, rolling over loosely until he came to rest finally at the bottom of the slope. There he lay on his stomach, head down, apparently dazed, as Lester, dragging his spooked horse after him, pursued Longarm down the slope. Longarm heard the horse gallop past him, and then Lester's heavy breathing as the big man bent over him.

Longarm had lost his hat in the plunge. He felt Lester's fist close about his thick hair. With a vicious yank, the man pulled Longarm's face off the ground and twisted it around. Longarm kept his eyes closed and did not cry out, though the pain that shot through his scalp was excruciating.

With a brutal snort, Lester let Longarm's head drop back to the ground. He stood back for a moment, contemplating his unconscious prisoner, and then decided to wake him up. He started by kicking Longarm as hard as he could. A sharp dagger of pain sliced into Longarm's side and swarmed up under his ribs. Longarm groaned dutifully and started to shake his head.

Again the man bent close. This time he took Longarm by the shoulder and flung him over onto his back.

As Longarm rolled over, he thrust his derringer into Lester's face.

With an oath, Lester straightened up and took a step back. The look on his face was a mixture of indignation and fury. He seemed to be thinking that Longarm had no right at all to pull such a trick on him. His rifle was still in his hand. He levered a fresh cartridge into the firing chamber and raised the rifle calmly, aiming it at Longarm's head. Then he smiled contemptuously.

"You think that little pea-shooter is going to stop me, do you, mister?"

Longarm moved the derringer to avoid the rifle barrel and rested its tiny sight on Lester's right eye. "Don't mess with this pistol, Lester. It carries a .44 slug. Two of them. Put down that rifle."

"Like hell I will."

As Lester spoke, he steadied his rifle. Longarm saw the man's finger·tightening on the trigger. Unwilling to wait a second longer, Longarm fired. The slug entered Lester's right eye, transforming it instantly into a gaping red hole. Lester's head snapped back and its shape appeared to change slightly. Grimacing, Lester ducked his head to one side, then began to sag slowly to the ground, blood pouring from his nose and eye socket.

But his finger continued to tighten on the trigger. The Winchester went off, and though Longarm flung himself swiftly to the right, he was unable to escape the bullet, which tore into his left side. The next thing he knew, he was tumbling pell-mell down a steep slope into a gully. He came to rest abruptly, his head slamming into a boulder. For a moment he lost consciousness completely.

When he regained it, he lifted his head and looked about him. He saw Lester's mount quietly cropping grass before the stand of timber where Longarm had left his horse. He pushed himself erect and almost immediately collapsed forward onto one knee as his left leg gave way under him.

More carefully this time, he reached out to a sapling and pulled himself back up to his feet. His left side was numb and seemed to have grown an exceedingly heavy encumbrance. He glanced down and saw that his entire left thigh and pants leg were dark with blood. Reaching in under his coat, he felt his wound. As he did so, the spent slug clattered to the ground. The bullet had nipped through his left side. Great, Longarm told himself grimly. It was just a flesh wound.

Carefully, aware that the pain would begin soon and that he must make the most of the time he had, he worked his way back up the steep side of the gully until he found himself once again face to face with Lester. The man was sitting on the ground with his back to the slope, his rifle across his knees, his head resting back. The right side of

28

his face was a shocking blue, the lower portion covered with the blood that had exploded from his nostrils. Blue-bottle flies were already buzzing around his nose, and a few were cautiously picking their way into his right eye socket.

Longarm took the rifle from the man's dead hands, then reached closer, plucked his Colt from Lester's belt, and dropped it back into his own holster. Turning away from the dead man, Longarm searched the ground until he found his derringer. Clipping it back onto his watch chain, he reached into the side pocket of his frock coat, selected a slug, and dropped it into the pistol's empty chamber. Then he carefully dropped the derringer back into his vest pocket. Blinking dazedly, he looked about him.

He felt suddenly woozy. His motions seemed unduly slow and deliberate, as if he were moving in a dream. Looking toward the timber, he saw Lester's horse still cropping the grass peacefully. He shambled across the flat toward the animal. As he got closer, the horse looked up at him, its ears twitching. Abruptly it nodded its head emphatically, swung around, and galloped off, its reins trailing.

Longarm held up, discouraged, his head spinning. The pain from the wound in his side was growing sharper. It felt as if a small animal were gnawing its way deep into his vitals. He became aware that his mouth was as dry as an old newspaper. He had to force himself to think.

His own horse was still inside the timber, he reminded himself. What he had to do was find it, then ride out, back to Red Gap if he could make it.

He started up again, lurching crazily until he reached the timber. Once he was among the cool trees, he felt a little better, and using the tree trunks for support, he continued on through the cool green aisles, slipping more than once on the slick pine needles.

As he continued on, he came gradually to realize that the crack he had taken on his head when he landed in the gully had opened his scalp. A large dollop of blood was slipping down over his left eye. When he reached up to brush it away, he discovered matted hair and a flap of peeled-back scalp.

He kept going and, after what seemed an interminable

time, came to the small meadow where he had tied up his animal. Staggering into the meadow, he looked about frantically.

His mount was gone!

He closed his eyes and tried to concentrate. Could he be sure this was the right meadow? The timberland must be filled with these small grassy oases. And then he saw the small brook. Yes, this was the right meadow, all right. It had to be. So where, then, was his mount?

A twig snapped behind him.

He flung himself around, bringing up the Winchester as he did so; but he only succeeded in throwing himself to the ground. Reaching out groggily to support himself, he felt the Winchester slip from his grasp. Groggily he raised his head to see who it was. But he could no longer see out of his left eye. He twisted his head around and caught a glimpse of something dark rushing toward him. Reaching across his belly, he drew his Colt and raised it.

A heavy boot caught his fist and knocked the Colt flying. Longarm put his head down and flung himself at his assailant's legs. Wrapping his arms around them, he brought the man down and began pummeling him wildly. But it was like punching a huge pillow filled with chicken feathers— and Longarm's arms had suddenly become as heavy as crowbars.

At last he gave up the unequal struggle and let himself drift off into sweet oblivion.

Chapter 3

Someone nearby was smoking one of Longarm's cheroots. Longarm opened his eyes and found his gaze resting on a tall, husky-looking fellow who was facing away from him, peering intently down a long slope, the cheroot's smoke trailing back over his hefty shoulders. A single red band circled his black shoulder-length hair. He was dressed in a fringed deerskin jacket, and matching pants tucked into black high-topped boots.

Longarm remembered where last he had seen one of those boots before—when it had been used to kick the Colt out of his hand.

He stirred himself carefully, aware of a heaviness in his side, but no great pain. He was lying under a pine tree on a slope, a buffalo blanket thrown over his body, a rough pillow of fragrant pine boughs under his head. He lifted his hand to his scalp and found to his astonishment that the flap of skin he remembered as having been peeled back was now solidly in place.

The Indian turned and looked down at Longarm, as if he had known all along that Longarm was fully awake. He took the cheroot from his mouth, hunkered down, and gently placed the lit cheroot into the lawman's mouth.

"Smoke," the Indian said. "I use it to call you from the sleep. You have slept enough, I think."

Longarm pushed himself to a sitting position and puffed on the cheroot. "And who might you be?" he asked, his head spinning slightly from the sudden exertion.

"Frank Fools Crow." He was a very handsome Indian, between thirty-five and forty years old, Longarm judged. His mouth was wide and expressive, his nose a sharp blade. His forehead was high, his brow craggy, as if it had been shaped carelessly with a chisel, and peering out from under it, his large, dark eyes—set well apart—looked deeply into Longarm's own eyes, as if he were looking for the roots of Longarm's soul.

"You're the one I tried to wrestle to death," Longarm said, recalling his last moments of consciousness before he passed out.

The Indian allowed himself a smile. "Yes. You were very weak. But very brave."

Longarm took the cheroot from his mouth. "You saw what happened?"

"I followed you from the timber. I saw Lester capture you." He smiled. "That is a very small cannon you have. But it works fine."

"How long have I been unconscious?"

"Your spirit fled your body for seven days until I called it back. Then you slept for two more days. Now your body has healed."

Longarm was startled to learn that he had been out of action for that length of time. He had considered the wound in his side as only a flesh wound. The blow on his head must have been much more dangerous than he had realized. "My scalp," he said, touching it gingerly again. "You've sewn it back together, I see. Thanks."

The Indian patted a buckskin pouch. "I learn to sew skin many years ago, from very famous medicine man. A true *pejuta wicasa*. There will be no scar."

Longarm stirred himself deliberately, testing his side. It

32

was slightly sore, but there was still no pain. "And the wound in my side?"

Fools Crow shrugged. "It took much *pejuta*," he said.

Longarm knew what he meant by that. Herbs, the wild herbs these Indians used as medicine. Their medicine men seemed able to cure a remarkable variety of injuries and illnesses with their odd herbs and salves—except, of course, for those plagues brought into their lives by the white man.

Fools Crow smiled. "You do not remember this?" As he spoke, he reached into his pouch and withdrew a sacred rattle. "This *wagmuha* keep you awake one night. You try to take it from me. Your spirit very angry at my spirit. It want to fly away to the *mahpiya*."

"The what?"

"What you call heaven."

Longarm took the cheroot out of his mouth and regarded Frank Fools Crow solemnly for a long moment, as he digested what the Indian was telling him. If what the man said was true—and Longarm saw no reason to doubt it—this Indian had saved his life.

"You are Shoshone?" Longarm asked finally.

"No. Lakota."

Longarm frowned. If Frank Fools Crow was a Western Sioux, he was a long way from home. "This is Shoshone country. What are you—a Lakota—doing here?" Longarm asked.

"My mother was Lakota. My father purchased her from the Sioux. He trap many beaver in these mountains. We live here with my brother and sister until my mother and father die in a great snow. After that, we return to my mother's people and I go on my first *hanblechia*, my first vision-seeking. When Crazy Horse call for braves to fight the horse soldiers, I became a true Lakota again. Now, after Long Hair's death at the Greasy Grass, I come back to the mountains of my father. I am not a reservation Indian."

Longarm nodded. If Frank Fools Crow had no taste for agency life, Longarm could not blame him. There were, Longarm knew, many pockets of renegade Sioux still remaining south of the Canadian border, having refused to follow their war chiefs into reservations or go north into Canada with Sitting Bull.

"I find your badge," Fools Crow said. "You are white policeman. So now you help me. Like I help you."

"Help you?"

Frank Fools Crow nodded solemnly. "I see you kill the man I want to kill. You are brave man. I am brave man. I fight with Crazy Horse at the Greasy Grass. Now we fight together."

"You mean you have another massacre in mind?"

Frank Fools Crow smiled, transforming his solemn, craggy face into sunlight and clear vistas. "That was not a massacre. Long Hair was a fool. He attack our camp. Our many braves swallow him up like a river swallows a handful of pebbles. Besides, the Lakota do not know how to massacre the way the white man and his Indian friends do." Frank Fools Crow looked closely at Longarm, his eyes alert. "Can it be you do not know I speak the truth, lawman?"

Longarm had no desire to argue with his Lakota benefactor on such a topic. "Just what is it you have in mind, Fools Crow?" Longarm asked, sitting up and pushing himself back against the pine. As he did so, he saw that the two of them were on a knoll that overlooked a cabin bordering a mountain stream well below them.

"My brother and sister have been taken by Simpson Radley," Fools Crow said. "This man Simpson is the father of the man you killed. He has many acres of land with tall grass growing on it, and he needs many people to help him cut the grass and pile it onto wagons. So he came to my cabin and offered us much paper money if we work for him. When we say no, he take us anyway. But I escape. Now Black Elk and Sits Tall Woman must stay and work for him anyway. Only they must work with chains. I have told Radley I will kill all of his people if he does not free Black Elk and Sits Tall Woman."

"You told him?"

Fools Crow's eyes went cold. "I told his man, Withers—after I cut off part of one of his ears. I told him if he would not tell Radley what I said, I would cut off the rest of his ear next time."

34

"Fools Crow, are there two white men also being forced to work for Radley? I heard Bob and Tim MacLaggan mention something about it."

"The two revenuers?"

"Yes."

"I have heard of them, yes. But I do not know if they are there still."

"And you were after Lester Radley when I happened along?"

The Indian nodded. "Will you help Fools Crow?" the Indian asked.

"Depends. First things first. What about Lester's body? Have the Radleys discovered it yet?"

"I hid it before I came after you in the timber. Then last night I dumped his body before Radley's door."

Longarm winced. Lester's body must have been fairly rank by that time.

"I wanted the Radleys to discover the body as soon as I left it," Fools Crow said. He smiled then, a cold, mirthless smile. "So I cut off Lester's two ears. I put them in a medicine pouch and send it through one of their windows. After this I give the war cry of my people and ride out of their yard."

Longarm gave this grisly tale some thought. Those two MacLaggans would have told the elder Radley that Lester had left with Longarm on his way back to their farm. When Lester had not shown up, they would more than likely have concluded that Longarm had escaped and, in the process, probably injured Lester—or worse. Now, however, they would most assuredly blame the Indian for Lester's death.

Which was precisely what Frank Fools Crow wanted, it appeared.

"You have quite an interest in ears, Fools Crow."

The big Indian shrugged.

Longarm glanced past him down the slope. "And that, I suppose, is why we are sitting up here instead of taking our ease down there in that cabin. You're expecting visitors. Is that right, Fools Crow?"

The Indian nodded.

"How soon do you expect the Radleys?"

"Very soon, I think."

"Then we'd better get the hell out of here."

"Your horse is waiting. Do you think you can ride?"

"Do I have any choice? What's your plan, anyway? You aren't going to try to bushwhack the entire Radley clan, are you?"

"No. While Simpson Radley is here with his men, we will be at his farm. We will free my brother and sister."

"You think it will be that easy, do you?"

"Of course it will, lawman." Frank Fools Crow smiled. "I have the law on my side."

"How do you know Simpson and his men will stay here long enough when they find you gone?"

Frank Fools Crow smiled. "I have left a friend in the cabin. He will keep them here for a time, I think."

Longarm caught the gleam of mischief in Fools Crow's eyes. "What kind of friend?"

"An old friend. He has lived here many years. I call him Silver Hump."

"Silver Hump?"

"He is a grizzly."

Longarm was amazed. "In your *cabin?*"

Frank Fools Crow nodded.

"How the hell did you manage that?"

Fools Crow looked very pleased with himself. "A trick of my father's," he said. "I find much honey, spike it with whiskey, then lead Silver Hump into cabin with this honey. He has eaten much and is now asleep. The Radleys will wake him up."

Chuckling at the thought, Longarm pushed himself to his feet. He shook his head to chase a momentary dizziness. "I just wish I could be around to watch all the fun," he said.

"That cannot be," Fools Crow said, a bit regretfully. "Come. This way to the horses."

With Fools Crow in the lead, they rode along a narrow ridge, heavily wooded with tall pines and firs. The going was slow as they wound their way through the heavy timber, and Longarm wondered at Fools Crow's selection of this trail, since at this rate it would take them one hell of a long time to get to the Radley farm, even if it was but a few miles farther on.

Abruptly, Fools Crow pulled up and motioned to Longarm to be quiet. Then he pointed to a meadow below the ridge.

Longarm looked and saw nothing. Then he heard the dull thudding of many hooves. A moment later, eight riders swept into view. The one in the lead had a long beard, a black broad-brimmed hat, and a long, flowing frock coat that billowed out over his cantle. They were using their horses cruelly as they flogged them across the treacherous, stream-broken meadow. Looking neither to the right nor to the left, they soon swept out of sight.

Longarm glanced at Fools Crow. "The Radleys?"

The Indian nodded.

"That one in front. He's Simpson?"

Again, Fools Crow nodded.

Then he turned and nudged his horse carefully down from the ridge, and a moment later, with Longarm just able to keep up with him, the Indian was in full gallop. There was, it seemed, no longer any need for caution. The ruse had worked.

In less than an hour, Longarm and Fools Crow were riding through the hilly acres of barley the Radleys had planted. Longarm could see that already a few fields had been harvested, but there were many more acres that had yet to be cropped. He could imagine how difficult it must have been to work this thin, rocky soil, and how painfully slow it must be now to reap the barley that had ripened.

The Radley farm was a mean-looking, untidy collection of unpainted shacks, cabins, and frame dwellings. The main building was a two-story farmhouse set on a slight rise. It looked unfinished, and as Longarm rode closer, he saw that it had simply been abandoned in the midst of construction. All of the windows on the second floor, overlooking the unfinished balcony, were boarded up.

There were three or four outhouses perched precariously on the stony, uneven ground. Longarm could smell them before he reached the front yard. The bunkhouse was constructed of pine logs and appeared to be the most solidly constructed building of the lot—until Longarm rode into the yard and caught sight of the large hole in its shingled roof that had been mended with pine boughs and a rotting blanket. A blacksmith's shed and barn across from the bunkhouse were in equally poor repair. The fencing was in a pathetic state, serving for the most part only as an occasional, rotting obstacle.

There was only one truly sound building on the place, and it was toward this building that Frank Fools Crow rode.

It was a small, four-sided frame building with a high peaked roof. It looked like a miniature church or country school, except for the fact that it had no windows and its single door was constructed of iron, its massive heft resting on equally massive steel hinges.

Frank Fools Crow dismounted in front of the building and trotted up to the door, Longarm catching up to him as soon as his stiff body would allow. A huge lock secured the door's bolt. Fools Crow stepped back, raised his rifle, and fired, shattering the lock. Fools Crow flung the lock away, shot the bolt back, and tugged open the huge door.

The stench of unwashed bodies and overflowing slop jars momentarily staggered Longarm. He closed his eyes and shook his head, then followed Fools Crow into the black, noisome interior of what was obviously a prison.

In the dim light he saw three figures huddled along one wall. He caught the gleam of chains. There were manacles about the three prisoners' ankles and wrists. Long chains attached to them led up to a single great iron ring fastened to the wall high above their heads. Since the only light came from the open door behind him, Longarm had difficulty making out the individual faces of the prisoners. Fools Crow hurried toward his brother and sister, while Longarm approached a third person huddled in a corner—a woman in her early twenties with long, matted blond hair. There was no sign of the two Treasury agents.

The woman flattened herself against the wall as Longarm came to a halt before her. When he reached down to examine the manacle on one of her wrists, she pulled her arm back swiftly and covered her face, uttering a tiny cry as she did so.

"I am not going to hurt you," Longarm said as gently as he could. "We're here to free you."

The woman slowly lowered her arm. "Who are you?" she asked. Her voice was steady, her eyes narrowed in suspicion.

"Custis Long," he replied. "A deputy U.S. marshal. Now how are we going to get these chains off? Is there a key?"

"I don't know," she said. "They have never taken them off."

"Get up."

She got up quickly. Despite the heavy chains shackled to her wrists, she managed to brush her long hair off her face and back over her shoulders. Her dress was torn and filthy, but he could see that she had been in this condition only a relatively short time.

Fools Crow came over to them. "Grab the chains," he told Longarm. "We can pull them out of the wall."

Longarm took hold of the chains leading from the woman's wrists and ankles, Fools Crow taking the chains that held Black Elk and Sits Tall Woman. The two men looked at each other and, at a nod from Fools Crow, heaved backward.

The huge iron ring was pulled from the wall and the chains slammed, clanking, to the dirt floor.

"Good," said Fools Crow. "Now we can leave this stinking place."

At that moment, however, as they turned to leave the prison, the bright sunlight pouring in through the open doorway was suddenly blocked out.

"Well, well, well," said a deep but unmistakably female voice.

A huge woman was pushing her way into the place. She was carrying a bullwhip. Behind her, Longarm glimpsed the face of an old man peering around her bulk. He had a pitchfork in his hand.

As the two came to a halt in front of them, Longarm said, "I think you'd both better get out of our way."

"Who the hell are you?" the big woman demanded, not budging an inch. The old man took his place beside her, a sour scowl on his face, his pitchfork at the ready.

"I'm a lawman. And in case you two didn't know it, slavery has been outlawed."

"Damn your eyes. You've got no call to come messin' in our business," the woman said. "These here are renegade Indians—and a traitorous woman with all the morals of an alley cat. We're doing them a favor! We feed them and they get a chance to do an honest day's work."

"Out of the way, woman," said Fools Crow, stepping closer from behind Longarm.

The woman squinted in the dim light at Fools Crow. "Ah, it's you, is it, you murderin' half-breed!"

As she spoke, she unfurled her bullwhip. It didn't seem that she would have much room to use it in such close confinement, but she managed somehow, and before either Longarm or Fools Crow could react, the whip's tail was snapping at the Indian, its leather thongs fastening about his neck. With a powerful yank, the woman dragged the big Indian closer. He stumbled to one knee as he tried desperately to peel the braided leather from about his neck. At once the old man with the pitchfork advanced on him, obviously intending to impale him on its filthy tines.

With a cry, their chains dragging on the ground behind them, Black Elk and Sits Tall Woman flung themselves at the old man. Uttering a startled cry, he went down under their onslaught. The big woman turned to go to his aid. But as she did so, Fools Crow yanked the whip out of her grasp. Before he could advance on her, however, the tall woman whom Longarm had freed had flung herself on her. Using her chains as a whip, she began flailing furiously down at the now-cringing mountain of flesh.

It took a while for Longarm and Fools Crow to drag the three prisoners off the fat woman and the old man, but they managed finally and pushed the pair out of the building ahead of them.

"Get over to that blacksmith shop," Longarm told them, "and knock off these shackles!"

40

The couple led the way across the yard to the shop. It was the old man, still occasionally muttering to himself, who held the shackles steady with tongs while the big woman wielded the hammer and chisel. Fools Crow stood beside her, his dark eyes watching the woman closely, his big fist holding her mass of untidy hair as a warning.

As soon as the shackles had been broken apart, Fools Crow looked at Longarm. "What shall we do with these two?"

"Gag them and put them in their own prison."

The big Indian smiled. He found filthy, oil-stained rags on the shop floor and stuffed them with great enthusiasm into their mouths. Then he herded them swiftly across the yard, flung them into the stinking darkness, and slammed shut the door. Longarm followed with a beam and nails. With the back of a hatchet, he nailed the beam across the door.

"You should have killed them—Ma Radley, especially," the blond woman said bitterly.

Longarm looked at her. "Do you really mean that?"

She took a deep breath and hugged herself. "I guess not," she admitted wearily. "But something has to be done about Ma Radley and the rest of that clan of hers. They are worse than Indians!"

Then she saw the sudden light in Fools Crow's eye, and blushed.

"This here is Fools Crow, ma'am," said Longarm. "Your two fellow captives are his brother and sister."

"Oh," she said hastily, "I didn't mean it to sound like that—"

"Sometimes I think the whites have no heart and no courage, that they come to this land only to destroy and kill," Fools Crow told her gently. "But then I think of my father—and I shall remember the courage you showed just now, when you attacked that mountain of a woman. I think I am wrong to think of whites as all bad—and you are wrong to think all Indians are just savages."

"Yes," the girl said hastily, nodding her head in agreement. "You are right, Fools Crow."

"What's your name?" Longarm asked her.

"Annabelle Svenson," she told him. "I've got a small farm in the hills north of here."

"How'd you happen to get mixed up in this?"

"I helped two men escape the Radleys."

"Were they Treasury agents?"

"Yes. When the Radleys discovered I had helped them, they brought me here. I've been their prisoner for almost a week."

"We must hurry," said Fools Crow. "The Radleys will be back soon."

Longarm and Fools Crow found horses and enough saddles in the barn for the girl and the two Indians. He was not used to stealing horses, but he figured if Billy Vail ever questioned him on it, he'd simply remind him that whatever the three took from the Radleys, it was only payment due them for their labor.

The five of them were on a ridge well above the farm when the first member of the Radley party returned. It was obvious even from that distance that this man was grievously wounded. He was able to stay on his horse only until he arrived in the farmyard. Then he slipped from his saddle, took a few steps toward the farmhouse, and collapsed. The five watched without a word as the fallen rider lay unmoving in the dust of the yard.

A few minutes later, four more Radleys rode slowly into view. One of them was Simpson Radley. Their heads were drooping wearily over their saddlehorns. Once inside the farmyard, they dismounted, hurried over to the fallen rider, and carried the man into the farmhouse.

The five riders remained on the ridge and waited for the rest to show up. But it soon became obvious that those five riders were all that would be returning from Fools Crow's cabin. There had been eight men in Radley's party.

"Five riders," said Longarm to Fools Crow. "That's all."

The big Indian nodded impassively. "They woke Silver Hump. Now I must worry about my old friend. I go now to see how he is, lawman. What direction will you take?"

"Guess I'll take Annabelle back to her farm and see if

I can pick up the trail of them two Treasury agents. I suspicion I'm going to need all the help I can get from now on."

"I will leave you, then," Fools Crow said.

Longarm nodded and watched as the Indian pulled his horse around and set off along the ridge, Black Elk and Sits Tall Woman riding just behind him. Fools Crow's sister glanced back at Longarm and smiled. He waved to her, admiring the way she rode. Her name suited her well.

On the night that Longarm had tried to take Frank Fools Crow's sacred rattle from him—when his spirit would rather have flown away to heaven rather than continue to dwell within his fever-ravaged body—a woman rode into Red Gap not long after Smitty and his teamsters arrived with the mail and supplies for that week.

During the ride from Taylor's Ferry, she had kept well back but always within sight of Smitty's pack train. She had camped a good distance apart from them; and from her aloof, guarded manner, Smitty and his men concluded that it would be best to wait her out, to see what her play was before moving in. At last they realized what she was up to. She was using them to guide her to Red Gap.

As soon as Smitty had that figured out, he rode back to introduce himself and tell her she was welcome to ride along with them. But she kept her distance and, with impressive dignity and great courtesy, declined.

Smitty rode back to his men thoroughly impressed. The woman was obviously a Mex, but she had class and a regal bearing that prompted him to keep his distance. Her pack-horse was a big, solid chestnut, and she rode a full-blooded Arabian stallion, as black as midnight. It was a perfect match for her. She wore her long dark hair wound into a neat bun at the back of her head. Her hat was a black high-peaked sombrero. Under her dark vest she wore a white silk blouse. A black silk bandanna was knotted about her neck. A dark woolen split skirt and beautifully tooled riding boots completed her riding costume.

Except for the gold necklace about her neck, from which hung a gold cross.

The daughter of Diego Sanchez—Rosita Castelnueva Sanchez—was once again on the trail of the deputy marshal she still called Longman. And this time she would not let herself be fooled by him. She had enough money to hire whatever men she would need to help her track and destroy the dog of a gringo who had killed her father.

Chapter 4

As Frank Fools Crow rode back to his cabin with Black Elk
and Sits Tall Woman, he remembered the time many years
before when he was crouching in his vision pit, alone for
the first time in his life, shivering from the cold and the
fear—awaiting his vision.

*It was the fourth day of his lonely trial and he was almost
losing heart. Night was coming on. He was lightheaded and
dizzy from the fasting and the loneliness. The medicine man
had left with him a rattle, a pipe, and a bag of kinnikinnick,
tobacco made from red willow bark. To comfort himself and
restore his courage, he ran his fingers along the pipe's
smooth red pipestem. It comforted him. If Wakan Tonka
gave him a vision, he would become a medicine man. Then
he would keep the pipe and with it perform many ceremo-
nies. The smoke from the pipe would go straight to the spirit
world, and back down through the smoke and through the
pipestem to him would flow the power of the spirits. It would
make him a powerful healer, a yuwipi.*

This thought comforted him for a while as he busied

himself wrapping closer about him the brightly colored quilt his mother had made for him. The night grew darker, the sounds about him more ominous. Blackness crowded about him like the wings of a raven. He began to hear only the voices that came from within him, the voices of his mother's people. They seemed to come right through the earth. He could feel their souls entering his body, stirring in his mind and heart. The darkness deepened. He imagined the raven tightening its wings about him. He shivered in apprehension and tried to keep his teeth from chattering.

Then other sounds came to him: the cry of the wind, the whisper of the trees, animal sounds, the hooting of an owl. Sweat stood out on his forehead as he became aware of an overwhelming presence shouldering its way into the vision pit beside him. He turned his head and found himself looking into the luminous eyes of a grizzly. The animal's moist snout almost touched his forehead.

Fools Crow was so frightened that he turned swiftly back around, his bones turning to ice. He grasped the rattle the medicine man had left him and began shaking it furiously. The sound soothed him, but when he dared to look up again, he saw that the grizzly was standing above him, shutting out the sky, his benign face regarding Fools Crow with—could it be?—affection.

Then he heard a human voice, strange and very low-pitched, a voice that could not have come from any living being. As the words came to him, Fools Crow was no longer in the pit, but was striding swiftly along beside his powerful, shambling companion. They were high on a mountain, looking down on a mist-shrouded valley, a canopy of brilliant stars over their heads. The air was thin and bracing. Fools Crow felt his heart pounding exultantly.

The voice said, "You are sacrificing yourself to be a medicine man. In time you will be one. You will teach other medicine men. We are the animals that walk like men. We are a nation and you shall be our brother. You will never kill or harm any one of us. You are going to understand us whenever you come to seek a vision on this hill. You will learn about herbs and roots, and you will heal people. You *will ask for nothing in return. A man's life is short. Make yours a worthy one."*

At that moment Fools Crow felt his nagi, *his soul, surge through him like a flood. It filled him—all of him—and he knew at once then that he would become a* wicasa wakan, *a medicine man. His vision had come. You will know it, the medicine man had told him. You'll know if you get the power. And the medicine man was right. His vision had come and the power was surging through him.*

In that instant he found he was no longer striding beside the great bear. He was back in his vision pit, weeping with happiness....

Recalling that vision made Fools Crow uneasy. He could not help but remember the words of his brother, the grizzly: *You will heal people and you will ask for nothing in return. You will never kill or harm any one of us.*

But he *had* asked for something in return for his healing of the lawman, and perhaps Silver Hump had not escaped entirely the wrath of the Radleys. Fools Crow did not like to think on that as he guided his mount carefully along the trail that now left the pines and wound its precarious way along the ridge ahead of them.

Not long afterward, Fools Crow pulled his mount to a halt and gazed down upon his cabin. It was perhaps a thousand feet below them. And from that distance he could not see too much damage. The door was open and hanging crookedly on one leather hinge. But outside of that, the place looked quiet, almost peaceful—and there was no sign of Silver Hump's body. Still, he felt an uneasiness grow within him. It was as if the wind moving through the pines above him on the slope contained voices that warned him. He shuddered slightly and urged his horse on.

A dark cloud of flies brought him to the first body, sprawled in a small hollow at least a hundred yards from the cabin door. It was caught up in a thick tangle of orchard grass and blood. Silver Hump had apparently caught the fleeing man from behind and, with one giant swipe, crushed his skull. The blow had peeled the man's head back off his shoulders. Pulling up his mount and leaning over to gain a better view of the remains, Fools Crow thought he recognized what was left of the man's face. It was Lafe Radley, the youngest of the clan.

He leaned back in his saddle and looked about the field for further signs of Silver Hump's fury. When he saw none, he turned about in his saddle to face Black Elk and his sister.

"I am going to follow the trail Silver Hump left," he told Black Elk. "You and Sits Tall Woman go into the cabin. Clean it out and pack what you can. This is a dead place for us now."

Without another word, he left them and followed Silver Hump's bloody trail as it led up the slope and away from the cabin. He came to a grove where the Radleys had evidently left their horses. One horse was on its side, its neck torn. Young Jim Scofield was still in the saddle, his ribcage laid open, his hairless face still frozen, his blue eyes open wide, as he was caught trying to wrench himself out from under the fallen horse. From there, Silver Hump's trail led across a narrow meadow into a heavy thicket.

It was, Fools Crow realized, where the old giant had gone to die.

With a heavy sense of foreboding, Fools Crow dismounted and pushed his way into the thicket. Silver Hump was sitting up with his back to a tree, his face sagged forward onto his massive chest. There were two ugly holes in his chest, one just to the right of his heart, the other just under his collarbone. One wound alone would have been fatal. Fools Crow surmised that Silver Hump had suffered both wounds before going on his rampage. The desolating fury of his kills reflected the despair he felt at the knowledge of his onrushing death.

Fools Crow felt that same rage now, as if the still-furious spirit of Silver Hump had remained behind to guard the bear's body. As he stood looking down at the dead grizzly, Fools Crow heard the voice of Silver Hump's spirit. Like a weary sigh, it seemed to come from the wind that moved through the aspens' branches, as well as from the massive carcass sitting before him.

*It is your white soul that has betrayed you—and this,
your brother. No more shall you walk beside us on earth,
no longer will the smoke from your pipe reach us. Like your
white brethren, you will know only what your eyes see and
your ears hear.*

As the words faded, Fools Crow felt his *nagi* rush from
him, leaving him empty, powerless. He was no longer a
wicasa wakan. His medicine was gone. In that instant, Fools
Crow felt desolate, like a child again, a stupid, frightened
child of the world. He tried to speak, but no words came.

Dumb, shaken, he turned and left the thicket.

The third body—that of Dill Williams—was still in the
cabin, crumpled in a corner, his right arm and shoulder torn
from his body. Fools Crow glimpsed what remained of the
man's heart, enclosed within a pale, blood-streaked sac now
crawling with flies. There was a look of implacable rage
still stamped on Dill's brutal face. It looked as if he had
been sliced down the center by a telegraph pole, and only
a quick movement of his head had prevented it from being
crushed like an eggshell. There was a huge Walker Colt
still clutched in his left hand and another, smaller Colt on
the floor beside his bloodied right hand. It was those two
weapons, Fools Crow had no doubt, that had fatally
wounded Silver Hump. And that was fitting, he realized,
since of Radley's crew, this was the one Fools Crow hated
the most.

Despite the heaviness in his heart, Fools Crow allowed
himself to feel a quickening of satisfaction before turning
his attention to the damage that had been done to his cabin's
interior.

He had left the sleeping grizzly on the floor before the
potbellied stove. The stove had been ripped from its place,
the four pieces of stovepipe hurled to the far corners of the
cabin. The spilled soot blackened everything, settling on
every horizontal surface. Fools Crow's sleeping blankets
in the corner were trampled and torn, their bright designs
fouled by blood and soot. A table and three cane chairs
were in pieces. Even a heavy oaken bucket had been
smashed to kindling. His tin cups and plates were scattered

everywhere. Black Elk and Sits Tall Woman had already taken out everything of value, leaving only this pitiable shambles. But they had not been able to save much, as he had already noted. Now, standing in the center of what was left of his cabin, Fools Crow had no difficulty at all in imagining the titanic struggle that had erupted when—undoubtedly shooting as they came—the six men had stormed into his cabin.

He turned and left. Black Elk and Sits Tall Woman were waiting for him beside the small pile of belongings they had saved from the wreckage.

"Burn the cabin," he said to Black Elk. "We ride out now. You and Sits Tall Woman take what you want. Go to Canada. Find Sitting Bull. You will be safe with him. I will stay in these mountains."

"We will not leave you, Fools Crow," said Black Elk.

Fools Crow looked at Sits Tall Woman. Her eyes were as defiant as her brother's.

"You do not understand," Fools Crow explained patiently and without anger. "I was foolish to do what I did. I thought Silver Hump would scare them, and the Radleys would turn and run in terror. They ran, but not before wounding Silver Hump. Now Silver Hump is dead. I must finish what he has started here. I cannot do this if I ride with you. Already you can see what my concern for you has led me to do. You must go from me. If you do not go to Sitting Bull, then leave this place and find another. And do not come back for me. Before another moon, I shall be dead."

He spoke this last without sorrow or regret, but as a statement of fact. The two looked long at their brother, saw that he meant what he said, and nodded dutifully.

"We shall go north," said Black Elk, "deeper into the mountains. If we find Sitting Bull there, we will join him."

Fools Crow nodded. "Good," he said. "Now we burn the cabin."

Dennis MacLaggan was at the kitchen table, taking a second cup of coffee after his supper, when Tim hurried into the kitchen to fetch him.

50

Glenna, the elder MacLaggan daughter, was at the sink washing the dishes, while Enid, her younger sister, dried. Glenna was as tall as her father already, with a tawny mane of reddish hair that flowed down her back as far as her waist. She had the gaunt face and high cheekbones of her tribe as well, and her father's sky-blue eyes. She was nearly twenty and filling out nicely. Enid, going on eighteen, was built more on the lines of her mother, with thick auburn curls, a patch of freckles over her broad cheeks, and piercing dark eyes. It hurt MacLaggan every time he looked into those eyes and saw his dead wife looking out at him, but he never let it break the smile he always had for his youngest.

Glenna turned from the sink at Tim's hurried entrance, and was about to say something sharp to her brother about tracking mud into the kitchen—until she saw the look on his face.

"What is it, Tim?" MacLaggan asked, frowning slightly. This quiet second cup of coffee in the kitchen, with his two daughters, had become a kind of ritual he looked forward to at the close of a day.

"It's Rad, Pa! He's ridin' in!"

"Simp Radley comin'? Has he got his barley in that soon, then?"

"More'n likely he wants us to give him a hand again, Pa."

MacLaggan finished his coffee and strode from the kitchen, Tim at his side. He held up suddenly, somewhat irritated at his partner's unexpected visit, until he caught a glimpse of Radley's face as the man rode into his yard. It was not only in the man's face. It was in the slope of his meaty shoulders, the almost negligent way he rode across the yard and pulled up before them.

"Light and set," Dennis MacLaggan said, not unkindly, a tentative smile on his long, craggy face.

"Thank you, Dennis," Radley said, dismounting wearily, his voice revealing an uncommon gentleness. MacLaggan perceived Radley's manner as a sign of trouble—bad trouble.

"Tim," said MacLaggan, with a nod toward Radley's

horse. At once the boy sprang forward, took the reins from Radley's hands and led the horse across the yard toward the barn.

"What is it, Rad?" MacLaggan asked gently. "You look and ride like you just came from trouble."

Radley took off his torn, misshapen hat, ran a pudgy hand over his thinning gray hair, and squared his shoulders, gazing at Dennis MacLaggan with lidded, bloodshot eyes. If Dennis had not believed it impossible, he might have thought he saw a trace of grief—tears, even—in the man's tiny eyes.

"I been peeled back and gutted," Radley said, his voice so heavy with grief that Dennis had trouble catching his words. "Then hung out to dry. I'm finished. Now all I want is help from you to get the two sons of bitches what done it to me."

"Whoa, there, Rad. Maybe you better come in and get some of that coffee I promised and tell me this a mite slower."

"I don't want just coffee, Dennis."

"We'll start with that, though. Now come on in."

Inside the kitchen, MacLaggan dismissed his two daughters with a quick nod of his head. Then he set out a cup for Radley and poured the coffee himself, after which he brought over an earthenware jug and planted it on the table between them. Radley slapped his hat down onto the table and poured a finger of moonshine into his coffee, then pulled the coffee up to his mouth. He swallowed the drink greedily, allowing some of it to dribble out of one side of his mouth. Then he reached for the jug and refilled his cup.

As he took a hefty gulp of the moonshine, he looked across the table at MacLaggan with the red-rimmed eyes of a man bent on murder. He was a sharp contrast to MacLaggan. While MacLaggan was a ruggedly tall individual with reddish-blond hair, eyebrows so light they barely showed, and eyes of a blue that astonished all who first looked into them, Simpson Radley was a short, dark, unkempt person, whose long, disordered gray beard and round, piggish face gave him the appearance of an unclean animal that had somehow managed to acquire a human's upright stance and power of speech.

Yet for four years, these two entirely dissimilar men had made a fine team. Radley grew the barley MacLaggan needed for his mash. MacLaggan provided the still and the nearly magical craft required to coax from it the best god-damn white lightning in the territory. They were too high for corn, but Radley had been able to pull steady crops of good-quality barley from his thin, stony fields almost without fail, despite a miserably short growing season. There was never any question about it; Radley and his clan had a tenacious hold on the earth, and were capable of wringing from it its last full measure.

"All right, Rad," MacLaggan said, "let's have it. What happened?"

"Lester," Radley groaned. "He's dead. And now Lafe's gone too."

"Gawdamighty, Rad. How?"

"That breed! Frank Fools Crow—working with that U.S. deputy what Lester took from your boys. I swear it must've been that breed what saved the deputy, then killed Lester. The breed carved him up some, then dumped him in my yard last night. The murderin' son of a bitch rode off yelling one of his heathen cries. He wanted me to know for sure who killed Lester. And when I went after him, he sprang his trap."

"A trap?"

Radley looked for a long moment at MacLaggan, as if he didn't know for sure if Dennis would be able to picture the situation properly. Then he took a deep breath. "It was a grizzly, Dennis. The biggest damn grizzly I ever saw in my life. He was waiting for us in the breed's cabin. We shot the place up and busted in, and that bear was on us afore we knew what hit us." Radley took a gulp of moon-shine from his cup and shook his head. Then he glared across the table at MacLaggan. "That bear was a pure mountain of fury, Dennis. He sure as hell tossed us around. Somehow, Dill managed to get off a couple of shots with those two Colts of his, and caught the bastard in the chest."

Radley finished the moonshine in his cup. "But hell, that just woke up the damn grizzly. He ripped Dill near in half and then took after us as we ran out. Goddamn, that son of a bitch could fly. He caught Lafe outside the cabin and struck him down with one swipe."

Silently, MacLaggan refilled Rad's cup.

Rad reached for it and drank it down without a grimace. He might as well have been drinking cold tea. "We made it to our horses, but the bear pulled down Jim Scofield's horse, killed Scofield, and went after Miles. He took out a piece of his back. It's a fearsome wound. Ma's doin' her best, but I don't expect Miles to live this night out."

"Rad, you sure that half-breed done this? Why, hell, that bear just might have broken into that cabin looking for sugar just before you showed up."

Radley shook his head grimly. "No, Dennis, that damn grizzly wasn't in that cabin by chance. That breed knew what he was doing, all right. He drew me to his cabin with Lester's body. He knew I'd come after him. That bear was left in that cabin deliberate. It was waiting for us. Then, while we was tangling with that grizzly, he rode into my place with that deputy, big as life, trussed up Ma and Pa, then freed his brother and sister and that whore. That's how they planned it."

"Did they hurt your folks any?"

"They gagged them and locked them in the guardhouse I rigged up. Ma said that Svenson girl tore into her when she was freed, then took a real delight when the breed gagged her and Pa. I'll get that bitch too. Don't you worry."

"I hate to say this, Rad, but I told you it was bad business, forcing that breed's brother and sister to work for you."

"I needed the labor, dammit! We ain't got much time before the rains. This could be the best crop of barley we've ever grown—"

MacLaggan reached over and patted his partner's hand. "Sure, Radley. I understand. But it doesn't matter all that much now, does it?"

Rad looked for a long, bleak minute into Dennis's eyes as he absorbed the impact of MacLaggan's words. Then he shook his head miserably and finished off the cup of moonshine. Abruptly he laid his head down on the table and began to sob. Loudly. The walls of the kitchen reverberated. It was a shocking sound that came with such suddenness that MacLaggan felt at first only the embarrassment any man feels when he is called upon to witness another's unashamed outpouring of grief. He covered up as best he could by leaning over and patting Rad on the shoulder; then he got to his feet and left the kitchen, closing the door softly behind him.

Even outside, with the door shut firmly, Radley's grief reached into the yard. Slowly, out of the gathering darkness, Bob and Tim approached him, the blacksmith and the wrangler behind them. Bob's gangling figure came to a halt in front of MacLaggan.

"What's wrong, Pa? That a man in there crying?"

"That it is, Bob."

"Simpson Radley?"

"I *told* you who it was!" insisted Tim, his blue eyes wide with anger that his brother should have doubted his word.

"It's Rad, all right," said MacLaggan. "He's in a bad way. I'll fill you in later."

The sobbing had died down by this time. MacLaggan turned and went back inside the kitchen. As he approached the table, he saw his two daughters huddled in the doorway. He beckoned them back out of sight with a wave of his hand, then sat down across from Radley. The man, still wracked by occasional sobs that silently shook him, was intent on filling his cup again. His hand shook slightly, but he didn't spill a drop as he lifted the cup to his lips.

Looking up at MacLaggan, he asked, his face mean now, his eyes gleaming with malevolence, "You goin' to help me get that breed—and the rest of them?"

"Go on back to your place. See to Miles. Maybe you should take him to town so the doc can look at him. And—you'll have some bodies to bury, won't you?"

"Yes. I'll have some bodies to bury."

"We'll help with that."

"But you won't help me get—"

"I didn't say that. First things first. You've got a crop to get in. My boys will help there too. And I'll have to shut

55

down the still, bleed off the rest of that mash. It'll be a loss, but there ain't no help for it, as far as I can see. Then we'll see about that breed and the marshal. Seems to me it would be in Smitty's interest to throw in with us this time. But we got to go careful, Rad. The killin' of them revenuers has brought one federal marshal. The killin' of another is going to bring in the army next. We got to do this right."

"I *told* you! I didn't have nothin' to do with that. Them revenuers was mutilated, remember. Just like Lester! That damn breed! He's the one did it! And with that deputy throwin' in with him, he ain't got a leg to stand on."

"But why would the breed kill them?"

"How the hell do I know? But everyone knows they was mutilated. And I wouldn't put anything past that breed. Not after this. Not after what he just done!"

"What about them other two revenuers we caught prowling around a couple of weeks ago, the ones we handed over to you?"

"They escaped. We went after them and thought for sure we had them cornered, but that whore bitch helped them get away." Radley's face showed a bleak, momentary gleam of satisfaction. "But Lester kept after them and tracked them into Beaver Pass. They was lost and bewildered and out of shoe leather by the time he caught up to them. No one's goin' to find their bodies, Dennis. Not the vultures and not the groundhogs. And that's the way them first revenuers would have ended up too, if we'd taken care of it."

MacLaggan sighed and nodded. There was nothing more to be said. He was Radley's partner—all the way. It didn't mean he had to like it, but it did mean that he had to square his shoulders, hitch up his britches, and put his shoulder to the wheel. And it didn't matter what horse manure that wheel had to move through. Radley had been grievously used since this federal deputy started nosing around, and now, with him in league with that crazy Sioux breed, there was nothing he and Radley could do but go after them—and the devil take the consequences.

MacLaggan stood up. "All right. Go on back and see to Miles. And do what you can to bring in the rest of that crop. I'll send my boys over as soon as I can. Then, like I said, we'll see to that deputy marshal and the breed."

Radley pushed himself erect. In the past half hour he had wolfed down nearly the entire jug of moonshine, but he stood before MacLaggan without wavering. The only sign of what he had consumed was a darker hue to his face and the brighter red rimming his small, mean eyes.

"I'll hold you to that, Dennis," he said heavily. "And much obliged. I'll be ridin' back now. The sooner you send your boys over to help us with the rest of the crop, the more I'll appreciate it."

"I understand, Rad."

Radley slapped his disreputable hat back onto his head, turned, and started from the kitchen.

"Wait a minute," said MacLaggan, snatching up the jug and following after him.

Radley paused at the door.

"Here," MacLaggan said, handing the man the jug. "Finish it."

Without a word, Radley took the jug and strode out of the kitchen ahead of MacLaggan.

Chapter 5

"Oh, Longarm!" Annabelle cried, falling back upon Longarm and turning her head away.

He held her gently, comforting her as best he could while he looked about him. He could not help but wince at what he saw. There had been some warning of what to expect as they rode up. Both windows had been smashed, and the door was sagging open on its one remaining hinge. Even so, there was no way either of them could have been adequately prepared for the mindless, systematic devastation that had been visited upon the interior of Annabelle's cabin.

The table had been smashed down the center, its legs ripped off. All the chairs had been stomped to kindling. An upholstered chair in the corner near the fireplace had been ripped open, its upholstery strewn over the floor, and its frame stuck into the fireplace, where most of it had been consumed by fire. Great, gaping holes had been chopped out of the wooden flooring. A large mahogany china closet had been pulled away from the wall and flung onto its side. Its glass doors had been twisted from their brass hinges, their panes shattered, the flooring about it ankle deep in shards of shattered china.

The shelves over the kitchen sink were hanging down, the wall cabinets ripped out, and all of Annabelle's cooking utensils, smashed and bent out of shape, were scattered about the stove and on the floor in front of the sink. The big black cookstove sagged crookedly where one of its small feet had been knocked loose; the stovepipe, trampled and misshapen, lay scattered over the floor, and soot now covered the kitchen area with a sad, black patina.

But it was the sight of the spinet piano along the wall beside the bedroom door that touched Longarm the most. It was this that had made Annabelle cry out, and was now causing her to sob quietly as she clung to Longarm. Longarm could imagine what it must have cost her in time and money and love to haul the piano this far into the wilderness. But she would play it no more. Shattered completely, it lay on its side, its legs broken off, its golden innards pulled out, the strings severed by what must have been the repeated blows of an ax. The ivory keys were scattered about the floor, the keyboard itself having been sliced through in two places.

A glance through the open bedroom doorway revealed a destruction as complete as that in the kitchen and living room.

"There's no need for us to go in any farther," Longarm told Annabelle. "Later, maybe. But not right now. We can camp outside for tonight."

Annabelle nodded dumbly and looked up at him through swollen, tear-stained eyes. "But first I want to go into the bedroom. There's . . . a music box."

"All right," he said, releasing her.

Eyes averted, Annabelle moved swiftly through the carnage, into the bedroom. Longarm followed her, pausing in the doorway to watch as Annabelle searched through the shambles of her bedroom. The dresser had been tipped over, the contents of its drawers strewn over the floor, its mirror shattered, the gleaming splinters ground brutally into the silk finery and dresses that had been folded neatly in the drawers.

Swiftly, carefully, uttering tiny cries of despair at what she found, Annabelle picked through the mess. At last, behind the overturned dresser, she found what was left of the music box. Its top was missing and the little, gleaming keyboard had been trampled underfoot with maniacal thoroughness. With unashamed tears in her eyes, she held the mangled music box up for Longarm to see.

"Do you think—I mean, could it be fixed, Longarm?"

"No," Longarm told her. "Leave it, Annabelle."

She nodded resignedly, placed it back down on the floor, then carefully rummaged around among the wreckage until she had managed to retrieve some clothing and other valuables. Wrapping these in a blouse, she got up and walked out of the bedroom past Longarm, fresh tears streaming down her face.

Half a mile from the cabin, Longarm found a brook that ran lazily through a meadow below a pine-crested knoll. Well in under its protective wing, close by one of the brook's lazy meanders, Longarm proceeded to build a campfire.

Disconsolate, sitting with her back to a sapling, Annabelle watched him. She had offered to help him, but he had insisted on her staying put; and she had done so willingly, allowing the tears to wash through her until at last she knuckled her eyes dry and looked up at him, her face no longer trembling.

"I am going to bathe in the brook," she told him. "I'll put on one of the dresses I saved. I won't be long."

"Good idea, Annabelle."

She gathered up her things and disappeared around the bend. A moment later he heard her splashing about in the water. When she reappeared, it was close to dusk. He saw that she had combed back her long blond hair, revealing the fresh, clean lines of her face. In the dim light from the flickering campfire, her large hazel eyes gleamed at him with a haunting beauty from out of the deep hollows of her eye sockets. She smiled as she approached him, and he was struck at once by the expressive line of her mouth. Barefoot, she was wearing a long, gownlike dress of a light purple, with lace at the neck and at the sleeves. The dress, Longarm

61

realized, was all she was wearing. She dropped lightly to the ground and curled up beside him.

"How do you feel?" he asked her.

"Better. But I'm famished."

"Supper coming up," Longarm said, reaching for the frying pan.

Black coffee, salt pork, and some biscuits were all he had been able to manage, but Annabelle swore it was delicious and ate ravenously.

Afterward, the fire dying at their feet, Annabelle told him her story.

Married in St. Louis to Carl Svenson, a man of twenty-two, she and her husband had set out three years before, overland to California, to look for gold. Once they arrived, however, they found the fabled gold fields already pretty well played out and abandoned. Undaunted, her husband decided he would seek his fortune in the Idaho Territory as a hunter and fur trapper. After building their cabin, Carl sold to a settler in the next valley the oxen they had purchased in St. Louis, and with the proceeds he bought himself a considerable array of hunting gear—firearms, traps, and packhorses. His career as a hunter and trapper, however, was no more successful than his career as a gold miner; once again Carl was too late, working over land that had long since been stripped clean or trapped out. Furthermore, he was a terrible shot and could never seem to keep track of where he had concealed his traps. Whenever he did eventually rediscover them, he found that wolves or bears had long since robbed them of whatever profit he might have realized.

And the winters wore him down terribly. Before the first winter was over, he had lost two fingers from his left hand, and one of his toes. He took to drinking during the long, howling blizzards that all but buried the cabin—and no amount of loving attention or cajolery on the part of his wife seemed capable of stirring him out of the black moods that descended upon him at such times.

She withdrew from him as a result. They quarreled. He

took to beating her. At such times he became a total stranger, staring across the dim cabin at her with fevered, disordered eyes, while outside the demented wind raged, battering furiously at the little cabin.

The second winter was their last. The storms descended once again, and Carl's inability to find his traps or shoot fresh game goaded him to a frenzy. By December he had taken to the cabin permanently, a raging, caged beast of no use to himself or his wife. At last, after a week of steady drinking, in the midst of a howling blizzard, he uttered a terrible cry and came after her with an ax. She fled out into the storm with him on her heels. In the swirling snow she lost her way, stumbled about for what seemed an interminable time, and then, through luck alone, found herself stumbling against the cabin's wall. She groped for the door, found it open, tugged it shut behind her, and with numb fingers rebuilt the fire in the fireplace.

Only then did she realize it was Christmas Eve. She sat by the blazing fireplace, a pot of hot coffee on the stove, and waited for her husband to return.

He never did. She found him late in January, frozen solid, sitting up with his back to a sapling less than a hundred yards from the cabin, the ax still clutched in his hand.

Annabelle went silent. She took a deep breath, tucked her knees up closer to her face, and hugged them, staring into the campfire.

Longarm did not prod her. He had heard this story before, in countless variations. Her husband, Carl, had been the typical young buck, not yet dry behind the ears, his head filled with Ned Buntline foolishness, newly married, journeying west to make his fortune. A pilgrim with no real resources, he had been devoured at last by the harsh realities of this fierce land—leaving his wife behind to pick up the pieces. Longarm always pitied the wan, pathetic women he saw bound to such errant fools. Annabelle, at least, was lucky. She had escaped with her life.

"As soon as I could," Annabelle said, speaking up again, "I made my way to Red Gap. Marge Pennock had told me the summer before that I could count on her hospitality if things got too bad for me." Annabelle smiled wanly at Longarm. "She was as good as her word, but I hadn't realized what she had in mind."

"Oh?"

"I thought she meant helping her with the hotel and the post office."

"That wasn't what she had in mind?"

"No. She has a part ownership in the Red Gap, the town's only saloon. She put me to work there."

"Selling drinks?"

Annabelle looked into Longarm's eyes. "Yes—among other things."

"I had a suspicion she might have run more than post offices before lighting in Red Gap."

"I didn't protest all that much, Longarm. It meant warm beds and eating regularly, and times—before the night crowd came in—when I could freshen up, stay in my room alone if I wanted, with no one to bother me. To heal, Longarm. In time I found I could choose the men I wished to pleasure. And after Carl, that was something."

"I suppose."

"When you are married to a fool or someone you loathe, Longarm, you have no recourse," she told him with bleak bitterness. "You have to make love to him—even though every nerve and muscle in your body is screaming out against the horror of it. At least in Red Gap, I had a choice."

"Then how did you come to be out here when those two revenuers came by?"

"In Red Gap I had a choice, not only over whom I would sleep with, but also my price. I did not tell Marge Pennock what I was charging." She smiled. "And my clients would not tell, either, for if they did, they would not enjoy my favors any longer. And they knew that. So after a while I had enough money salted away to leave Red Gap."

"And set up here?"

"Yes. I had a few friends who visited me and who generously repaid me in ways they felt appropriate. Meanwhile, I was able to farm this land enough to provide for my immediate needs. I was still healing, Longarm. Still reveling in the freedom I have enjoyed since Carl's death."

"And then along came the revenuers."

"Yes," she said grimly, brushing her hair out of her eyes with a sudden angry gesture. "I gave them food and beds to sleep in. I was outside when I heard Lester Radley and his men coming. I hurried back to the cabin and told the men to leave, that I would stall Lester for as long as I could."

"You just sent them away?"

"I told them to head for Beaver Pass and a settler I knew on the other side of it. I gave them directions." Then she shrugged wearily. "But they were terribly green, Longarm. Like Carl in a lot of ways. I don't know how far they could have gotten."

"And then you stalled Lester."

"Yes. He and his cronies came up to the cabin near sundown and surrounded it. When he yelled out, I told him I was busy and that my customers would come out when I was finished with them. That made sense to a fool like Lester, and he waited. When night fell, he got restless, like I knew he would. He fired a few shots at the cabin, so I opened the door and told them to come in. They stormed past me and I ran off."

"But they found you."

"They tracked me all that night and caught up with me in the morning. After they were . . . finished with me, Lester took after the two revenuers and I was brought back to the Radleys' farm." She looked wearily over at Longarm. "Now, for a while, I am a free woman once again."

"Only you don't have much to return to."

"No, Longarm. I don't."

"This settler—on the other side of Beaver Pass. How well do you know him?"

She blushed slightly.

Longarm understood at once. "He is one of your friends?" She nodded.

"How does he get along with the Radleys?"

"He loathes them. As well as the MacLaggans, and all

65

the rest of these wild, bootlegging clans that infest the mountains."

"You think he might look kindly upon letting you stay with him for a while?"

"He is married, Longarm."

"And his wife knows about you?"

"Of course not."

"Then if you and I arrived—as a couple—she would have no suspicion. I mean about you and her husband."

"I suppose not."

"She hasn't heard about you?"

"She stays on the farm. A lonely, solitary, taciturn woman. She knows no one. Harley likens her to an ox, a steady, dependable, silent beast of burden. She seems to live only for the children and the farm. He has given her that, Harley says, and she has made it clear to him that this is all she wants from him."

Longarm nodded. He had seen that too. Women so burdened with housework and a string of gaunt children that they became transformed into beasts of burden—and drove out of themselves all of the tenderness that once made them so sweet and loving to their husbands. They became red-knuckled martyrs to their families—but wives no longer.

"We'll set out for Beaver Pass in the morning," Longarm told her.

"All right," Annabelle said, sighing. "I suppose you're right. There's no sense in me going back—ever—to that cabin. It's about time I put it behind me."

"That does sound wise," Longarm said gently.

She looked at him, her face softening. "Why don't you . . . come closer, Longarm?"

There was no doubt what she meant. He smiled and reached out and patted her arm. "That's all right, Annabelle. You've had a long, tiring day."

It was as if he had struck her. "I see," she said. "You mean I am not clean. You do not want me to comfort you. I am a whore to you, and that is all I am."

"Whoa. Let's eat this here apple one bite at a time. I didn't say that."

66

"But it is what you meant. Longarm, do you know who had me last? The Radleys. Whenever they wanted. After the work in the fields, when I was too exhausted to fight them, they would come for me. It was horrible. You have no idea."

Longarm frowned. "You don't have to tell me this, Annabelle."

"But I want to tell you, so you'll understand why I just...why I suggested what I did. Don't you see? Just because one has been forced to drink at a pig's trough, it doesn't mean that one would not like a glass of fresh water."

"To clean you."

"Yes," she said. "Oh yes. I feel so dirty, Longarm. So used. But with you, I felt it would not be that way. You are clean. I like the honesty in your eyes, the way that mustache coils up, the strong, masculine scent of you—the smell of good leather and dust and sweat. I am not a wanton. But I need to feel whole again, free to choose my own man."

He smiled. "And you chose me."

She looked at him closely, measuring him, he thought. "Yes. I chose you. I was not offering myself as a favor to you, Longarm—a payment, as you thought. No, I am a woman who has been used cruelly and brutally, and I hoped that you would begin the healing. But there's no need for that now. I am sorry I made such a brazen request. I should have known better."

Longarm was deeply impressed—and not a little moved. Seldom had a woman spoken to him so openly of her needs. It was in sharp contrast to the many others he had known who always conspired to make it appear that they were doing Longarm a favor, that their own appetites in the matter were of no moment.

He reached out, took her gently in his arms, and drew her toward him. "No," he said quietly, as he smiled down at her. "*I* should have known better."

"Wait," she said, getting to her feet.

It was almost completely dark now, and the campfire had been reduced to glowing ashes. By its rosy light he watched her step out of her dress, and became aware of her golden pubic fringe gleaming in the midst of her shimmering paleness.

She knelt beside him and carefully, expertly undressed him. When he tried to help, she gently disengaged his hand. "No," she whispered, caressing his forehead with her lips. "I want to do it. Let me."

He did not argue, and soon he was naked and she was settling beside him, brushing her finger swiftly over his face. He felt the warmth of her long limbs pressing close alongside his. A moment later she was kissing him softly, her head moving only slightly, her lips parting his with a gentleness—a delicious, practiced restraint—that was almost a caress.

After a moment Longarm felt his senses reeling. Aware of his condition, she lifted her lips from his and gazed teasingly down into his eyes. "Mmm, Longarm. You taste so good."

He laughed and pulled her back down onto him again. Her breasts were full against his nakedness, their warmth startling him. He felt desire leaping up from his loins, and his kiss became urgent. She uttered a tiny laugh, then found his lips again. This time her gentleness vanished as she thrust her tongue with wanton abandon deep into his mouth. He wrapped his arms more tightly about her, enclosing her shoulders completely. Then he moved swiftly over her so that she lay on the ground beneath him.

She sighed, pulled her lips away from his, and began to nibble on his earlobe.

"Yes, Longarm!" she told him happily. "Oh yes! I'm ready."

Abruptly he decided it was his turn to tease. Chuckling, he moved his lips down her chin and began kissing the hollow of her neck. He heard her soft murmurs of pleasure and continued on down until his lips were moving over her breasts. Again he was astonished at their pulsing warmth. Biting lightly at her nipples, he flicked them delicately with the tip of his tongue and felt them harden.

His lips moved down to her belly, glided softly through

68

her moist blond curls, lingered there for a moment, then moved back up to her breasts. She was moaning softly by now, writhing beneath him. He was on his knees, straddling her, his erection pulsing eagerly as he continued to move his lips hungrily over her breasts.

She moaned, then lifted up her head and sank her teeth into his shoulder, biting almost hard enough to draw blood. In response he took one of her breasts in his mouth, roughly. Groaning in ecstasy, she spread her legs to receive him, then lifted her thighs. He felt the hot wetness of her, nudging hungrily against the tip of his erection. He could hold off no longer and plunged down into her, astonished and pleased to find her as tight as a clenched fist.

"Slow," she whispered huskily, her head back, the lines of her throat taut. "That's it. Oh, so nice and slow. Yes . . . !"

He did as she told him. Each time he felt himself nearing a climax, he forced himself to slow to a stop, plunging fully into her hot depths, holding her tightly and pressing in as deeply as he could without motion, impaling her fiercely on the ground. Her breathing eased and her moans died away until he began to thrust once more. At last she had had enough. She began to tremble from head to foot, and beat upon his broad back with her small fists.

"Now! Now!" she cried.

He laughed and stepped up his tempo, and soon all premeditation was gone. Annabelle began turning her head rapidly from side to side, her eyes shut tightly. Longarm lost all sense of time. The mindless rhythm of his thrusting achieved a life of its own—until with a grim, wild plunge, he drove deeply into her, driving her buttocks cruelly into the ground, and exploded.

Annabelle shuddered and let out a despairing groan that was almost a sob, then clamped herself even more fiercely about his pulsing erection. He felt her writhe uncontrollably. Again she cried out, but this time it was more of a scream than anything else as she came at last, pulsing wildly under him. He felt her juices flowing out around his erection. The scent of her became almost overpowering. Abruptly she flung herself up into his arms, hugging him to her, sobbing

69

uncontrollably and laughing too, all at the same time.

"Oh, Longarm," she cried. "I feel so...clean again. That was so good, so sweet!"

"Hush," Longarm murmured, lying back down and pulling her gently onto him. Stroking her sweaty hair, he kissed her softly on the cheek. "There's no need to talk. Let's just lie here and think on it. And rest up some. We got a long ride ahead of us tomorrow."

"Yes," she murmured, kissing lightly the wiry coil of hair on his chest. "Yes, Longarm. We'll just lie here and think about it. That would be nice. So nice."

She coiled her arms about him and hugged him contentedly to her as she rested her cheek on his chest. Stroking her hair idly, Longarm watched the stars gleaming above him for a moment, and was about to point them out to her when he became aware of her regular breathing—and realized that she was asleep.

Chuckling softly to himself, he continued to stroke her hair gently until he too drifted off.

Pulling up suddenly, Longarm swung off his horse, his eye riveted to the spot off the trail where he had caught the sudden, winking gleam of sunlight on metal.

"What is it?" Annabelle called, pulling up also and dismounting.

"I'll tell you in a minute," Longarm said, leaving his mount and picking his way swiftly down among the rocks. "It may be nothing at all."

He paused suddenly, studied the ground for a moment, then leaped a small gully, after which he knelt on one knee and peered closely down at a small patch of ground under a sandstone ledge. It was covered thickly with pine needles. Longarm began to pat the ground gently with his hand. He was about to give up when he felt something metallic mixed in with the needles. Gently brushing away the pine needles, he uncovered a Treasury agent's shield—one tiny point of which, a moment before, had winked at him in the noonday sun.

Annabelle was beside him by this time. He stood up and held out the shield to her. "Recognize this?"

She nodded. "It's a badge. Like the one the tall revenuer showed me when he and his friend entered my cabin."

Longarm nodded and glanced up at the rocks glowering down on them. Then he looked back at Annabelle. "Of course, there's no way I can tell now if this belongs to either one of them. But you sent them this way, didn't you?"

She nodded.

"And you say Lester Radley was on their trail?"

"But I never knew what happened after they took me back to their farm."

Longarm looked carefully down at the shield. It was not tarnished or rusted. He buffed it on his sleeve. The bright sunlight leaped from its surface. It had not been lying among those pine needles for very long, and no Treasury agent worth his salt would have parted with his shield easily, or left it behind if he could have returned to retrieve it.

Again, Longarm looked about him at the forbidding tumble of rocks and sheer walls that hemmed them in.

"Annabelle, have you ever been here before?"

"Yes, but not often."

"Can you think of anyplace where a body—or bodies— could be hidden easily? A cave maybe, or a steep gully."

She frowned in thought, then looked back at the trail they had just left. "Once," she said, "Carl got lost here. It was our second winter and there was a terrible blizzard coming up. I could feel it. So I went looking for him. I found him here, huddled in a cave. He had built a fire inside and was trying to warm himself over it. He wanted to stay there, but I wouldn't let him."

"Where's the cave?"

"Up there—I think." She was pointing to a ledge about twenty feet above them.

From where he was standing, all Longarm could see were low scrub pine, and beyond them a sheer wall of ribbed sandstone and granite.

"Show me the way up there," he told her.

She studied the terrain a moment, then hitched up her long skirts and moved nimbly ahead of him toward a clump of aspen. He followed her through the grove to a small game trail. It went both ways. She hesitated once again, then chose the steeper of the two. In a moment they were on the ledge, standing beside the scrub pine.

"I don't see any cave," Longarm said.

"That's funny," Annabelle said. "It's on this ledge some-where, I'm sure."

They were facing a sheer rock face. Scrub pine and birch grew along its base. But there was no sign of a cave.

"It looks so different now," she said, puzzled. "There was only the snow then, and the brush and these trees were covered. The smoke from Carl's fire showed me the way to the cave. I never could have found it if it hadn't been for that."

Longarm nodded and moved to the rim of the ledge, and began poking carefully through the scrub pine that covered it. He worked his way into a position that put him directly over the spot below where he had found the shield. When he reached it, he became even more selective and thorough as he searched through the scrub pine.

And in a few moments his diligence was rewarded.

He stood up, pulling into view a wallet. As he did so, bills spilled out. Opening the wallet, he found the spot where the agent's shield had been pinned. He took the shield from his pocket and carefully, easily placed the shield back in its proper place.

"Do you recognize this wallet?" Longarm asked Anna-belle.

She hurried over to examine it. "I can't tell, Longarm. Men's wallets all look the same to me."

He nodded and continued to look around. "That boulder," he said, pointing to one resting against the rock face farther up the trail. "Do you remember that?"

She squinted at it. "No I don't, but remember—it was so long ago and it was winter."

He walked up the trail to the boulder, Annabelle keeping pace with him, and found where the boulder had been rolled down from a higher level, then wedged close against the wall—fairly recently, judging from the amount of damage to the vegetation about it. The boulder was ponderous, but a strong branch would make an effective lever.

He poked his head in behind the boulder. In the shadows,

close to the face of the cliff, he caught sight of something familiar and reached down for it. His fingers closed about the rim of a battered derby—and as he pulled it into view, he saw a neat bullet hole in the crown.

"Hold this," he told Annabelle grimly, handing her the hat.

He found a dried-out, bone-dry branch farther up the trail, and used it to pry the boulder back from the wall. At last, when he found that he could push himself behind the boulder, he crouched down and started to search for the cave's entrance—then immediately pulled back, appalled, his senses reeling.

His search was over. He had found not only the cave, but the moldering remains of Dick Wilson and Tom Moon. The stench of their rotting corpses attested to that.

Chapter 6

It was Hale Murdock, one of Smitty's teamsters, that Rosita Sanchez selected to kill Longman—as she insisted on calling the tall deputy marshal. Rosita had approached Murdock in the Red Gap saloon and had made her offer almost without preamble. It was simple enough. Two hundred dollars in newly minted gold coins for the deed, with another three hundred due, once Murdock satisfied her that the lawman was dead. Murdock had accepted just as promptly. And when he had mentioned the possibility of taking Longarm's scalp as proof, Rosita had momentarily blanched, then swiftly recovered her composure and, with dark eyes gleaming, nodded her approval.

As Murdock studied the Mex woman, he decided quickly that he would not bother to tell Smitty of his sudden good fortune. There was no reason why he should split this bonanza with anyone else; especially since afterward, he was sure, he would find a way to separate this crazy Mex from all that gold she was carrying around. Of course, he would taste some of her delights first. That went without saying.

He didn't think he'd have much trouble taking her. The moment she sat down across from him and then leaned close to tell him what she wanted, he could feel the heat of her. Murdock understood perfectly. He was a tall, gaunt man who wore a red bandanna tied about his thick dark hair. A green eye patch covered his left eye, and a livid scar ran up his right cheek. This piratical appearance of his seemed to have an awesome appeal for some women. When they shook hands on the deal and he took Rosita's gold, he could feel her excited trembling increase, the closer his scarred face came to hers.

He told Smitty he was quitting in order to go hunting in the mountains. He knew Smitty suspected something, but he left before the man could do anything to stop him. And now he was perched high in a craggy nest of rimrock, watching Longarm and that whore, Annabelle, riding out of Beaver Pass into the high, lush valley beyond. It looked like they were on their way to Harley Cameron's place, the Bar C.

That might be where they were heading, but they sure as hell weren't going to get there—not today. Not ever. Trouble was, he was going to have to kill the girl too. And that made it a mite ticklish. He lifted his rifle and levered a fresh cartridge into the firing chamber. He decided he would knock the girl from the horse first; that would make it certain that the deputy would not go anywhere in a hurry. He would be too big a man to ride off and leave a fearfully wounded woman behind.

He smiled at the thought as he tucked the stock deeper into his shoulder and began to track the girl.

A split second before he heard the rifle shot, Longarm saw the tiny puff of dust that erupted from the horse's neck as the round struck. The animal went down almost immediately, carrying Annabelle with it. Her startled cry almost drowned out the second shot, which took Longarm's Stetson off his head.

He flung himself from his horse, snaked his rifle from its sling, then crabbed to Annabelle's side. She had been thrown clear, but was unconscious, her head resting alongside a boulder embedded in the ground. A quick examination revealed the swelling lump where her head had struck the boulder. He shook her, but could not rouse her. A third round plowed into the thrashing horse beside them. Cursing, Longarm took out his .44 and ended the animal's agony with a bullet through its brain.

Then he reached for his hat and turned his attention to the son of a bitch firing on him from the rocks above. The fellow obliged with a round that whizzed past his right cheek, then ricocheted off a rock behind him. Longarm dove for cover behind the dead horse's carcass, then looked about for his own mount. It was standing a considerable distance from him, its ears flicking nervously as it looked back at Longarm. At least it hadn't been hit. Longarm glanced back up at the rocks, and this time caught the glint of sunlight on a rifle barrel.

He saw a puff of smoke and ducked again. The rolling crack of the rifle shot echoed in the valley as the bullet whined past him and thudded into the ground. He heard Annabelle groan and reached back to keep her down.

"Stay where you are," he told her. "Don't sit up."

"My head," she groaned, attempting to sit up. "It hurts awful, Longarm."

"Lie still!" he told her, pushing her brutally back down.

She cried out angrily and started to resist when another round slammed into the ground near her, then whined off like a hornet. At once Annabelle stopped struggling and lay still.

"My God, Longarm!" she whispered. "What's happening?"

"Someone is shooting at us. Stay where you are while I go see who the hell it is. Don't move until I get back."

She just nodded as Longarm left the protection of the horse's carcass and began to worm himself through the grass toward the rocks. He was at least a hundred yards closer to the ridge before he was fired upon again. The slug slammed into the ground just in front of him, the sudden explosion of dirt almost blinding him. He hung back and dug the dirt out of his eyes, then started to pull himself through the grass again.

The next round struck the ground less than a foot from his right side. A moment later another one plowed into the sod inches from his waist, this one on the left side. Shit!

The jasper was bracketing him! Longarm leaped to his feet and raced for the rocks. Two quick shots came from above, but he heard neither round buzz past and kept going. One more shot plowed into the ground just in front of him—and then he was close in under the escarpment, hugging the rocks, at last out of the rifleman's line of fire.

Longarm calmed himself down for a moment, then began to scramble up the steep slope. He moved swiftly, aided as much by his low-heeled cavalry boots as by his enthusiasm to get his fingers around the throat of the son of a bitch up there. More than once he was forced to plunge his rifle's stock into the treacherous talus to keep himself from sliding back down the slope. He was aware that he was not moving very quietly, but he kept going, nevertheless, a controlled fury giving him the stamina of a mule and the agility of a mountain goat. At times his route was almost straight up, it seemed; but at last the ground beneath his feet began to level off. He slipped on some gravel, came down hard, scrambled to his feet, raced up the smooth face of an outcropping of granite, then ducked around a boulder.

He was met by a precisely swung rifle stock that caught him squarely in the gut, just below his waist. Longarm felt as if he had run full-tilt into a singletree. The force of the blow not only stopped him cold in his tracks, it lifted him a few inches off the ground before it sent him sprawling.

As Longarm slammed into the ground, he lost his rifle and immediately began to pull his legs close up under him. Then he began to twist slowly about, like a huge worm someone had just stomped on. He grimaced but refused to cry out. He felt the cold sweat standing out on his forehead, while the pain that swarmed up out of his gut caused every nerve and muscle in his body to scream out in protest. Through a red haze, he saw the scarred face of his assailant peering down at him. The man wore no hat, just a red bandanna tied about his head. A green eye patch covered one eye. As the man smiled, he activated a long, livid scar that ran up one cheek.

"No sense in my bothering to shoot you, Longman," he said, "if'n you're going to rush right up here so I can beat your brains out."

His laughter was closer to the bark of a scavenging coyote than to anything human, and Longarm suddenly remembered seeing him outside the hotel in Red Gap, with Smitty. This was one of Smitty's teamsters!

The teamster stepped closer and kicked Longarm. Hard. Longarm heard a groan break from his mouth, despite himself. He rolled over onto his stomach and hugged himself desperately. The teamster grabbed his shoulder and flung him around, then reached for Longarm's Colt. Examining the walnut grips, he stood up and hefted the weapon, then smiled.

"Thanks," he said. "This here's a fine-looking sidearm. You won't miss it where you're going."

"Who the hell are you?" Longarm managed through gritted teeth.

The man laughed, stuck Longarm's Colt into his own belt, then hauled up his rifle. "Your executioner, Longman."

"What'd I ever do to you?"

The teamster levered a fresh cartridge into the Winchester's firing chamber. "Nothing," he admitted, cheerfully enough.

Longarm had been writhing purposefully, his hand groping for his vest pocket and the derringer. Now he brought the weapon up, aimed swiftly, and squeezed the trigger.

The derringer misfired.

For a second the teamster pulled back, startled. Then, with a sudden howl of triumph, he stepped close and kicked the derringer out of Longarm's hand. The small weapon went sailing and slammed into the side of a boulder.

And went off.

The teamster froze in astonishment as the round whined past him. Instantly, Longarm flung himself on the man. Wrapping both arms around his legs, he grappled the teamster to the ground. In the struggle, the man lost his Winchester and tried to club Longarm with his own Colt.

But at close quarters, Longarm found his assailant surprisingly light—even fragile. He punched the man in the midsection, doubling him over. Another punch caught the man under the chin, straightening him up again. But the teamster managed to hang on to Longarm's Colt and tried to bring it up. Longarm stepped close, grabbed the wrist of the teamster's gun hand, and twisted violently. He heard and felt the man's brittle wristbone snap. The man fell to one knee, uttering a harrowing cry of pain.

Longarm stood over him, panting. "Now, damn you," he said, "who sent you?"

"My wrist! You broke it!"

"I'll wring your neck if you don't tell me what this is all about!"

Still clutching his shattered wrist, the man appeared to be in too much pain to concentrate on Longarm's words.

Grimly, Longarm took a step closer. The fellow's eyes widened in panic. Without warning he scrambled to his feet, turned, and raced for cover among the rimrocks. He ducked around the same boulder Longarm had come out from behind earlier. Cursing, Longarm raced after him.

And then came to a sudden halt.

Reaching out, he grabbed hold of a small sapling growing close to the boulder, and watched the teamster. The poor son of a bitch was scrambling to keep his footing as the pebbles under his boots continued to carry him inexorably closer to the edge of the slope. It was almost comical to watch him struggle to stay on his feet. But Longarm did not laugh. As the teamster reached a portion of smooth, sloping caprock, his legs flew out from under him—and he slammed down hard onto his broken wrist, howling in agony. Frantically he reached out for something to grab.

But his hand was of no use, and by this time his whole body was sliding swiftly over the caprock's devilishly smooth surface. The man screamed, turned halfway around, then hurtled backward off the rock and into space. Longarm heard the man's scream stop abruptly when his body struck the first time. Then his screaming began again as the man tumbled headlong the rest of the way down the slope. His ragged, hopeless shrieking ended suddenly when he came to a halt at the foot of the escarpment.

It didn't take Longarm long to find the teamster's mount. It was tied to a sapling not far from the ridge. Nor did it take him long to discover the two hundred dollars in gold in the man's saddlebags. This discovery gave Longarm pause. It occurred to him that perhaps this bushwhacker was, in reality, a hired assassin.

But who would possibly want to go to the trouble to hire such a pirate to bushwhack him? If the Radleys or anyone else in this high country wanted to do him in, they would simply take after him—as Lester Radley had taken after Dick Wilson and Tom Moon. Something the teamster had said—or rather, the way he had addressed Longarm—caught in his mind tantalizingly. He tried to recapture it, but he could not do so, not while he was filled with concern for the wounded Annabelle, waiting for him below the ridge.

Leading the teamster's horse, Longarm found a game trail that led off the ridge to the valley. When he reached Annabelle, he found her sitting up some distance from the dead horse, considerably woozy and still complaining of a terrible headache. He had to help her into the teamster's saddle, and it was only through sheer grit that she was able to keep up with Longarm as they rode deeper into the valley on their way to Cameron's Bar C ranch.

As soon as they rode onto Cameron's land, Longarm noticed how the rancher was coping with this high valley's awesome winters. Dotting the rangeland, he saw, were log lean-tos built by Cameron and already stocked with some hay in preparation for the coming winter, as Cameron saw to it that his beeves would never be far from feed, no matter how high the drifts were piled. As Longarm got closer to the ranch house, he saw also that Cameron was keeping his younger stock fenced into feedlots. As a result they were already putting on tallow.

Cameron was no fool, it appeared. He realized full well that to survive at this altitude, a cattleman had to be a farmer as well as a rancher, at least as far as taking care of his livestock was concerned.

They reached the Bar C late that same afternoon. As Longarm neared the compound, he saw a woman in front of the long, low cabin that served as the main house. She was washing clothes in a huge wooden tub, and four children—it looked like three boys and a girl—were skipping about her. Recently washed clothes hung heavily on a clothesline that ran from the corner of the ranch house to a pine. The woman straightened when she caught sight of them, and said something to the oldest of the boys.

The towheaded kid darted for the house. A moment later a man whom Longarm assumed was Harley Cameron appeared on the low porch, a rifle in his hand. He shaded his eyes and peered for a second or two at Longarm and Annabelle, then leaned his rifle against the house and left the porch in one quick stride. Longarm could hear him calling to his men.

Longarm reined in when Cameron reached him, then dismounted and helped Annabelle down. By this time, Annabelle had given up the struggle to remain conscious. The moment Longarm reached up for her, she simply collapsed into his arms. He caught her as gently as he could.

Cameron was obviously upset at Annabelle's condition, though he was careful, Longarm observed, not to let on that he knew the girl.

"What happened to this woman?" he asked carefully, as Longarm started to carry Annabelle toward the ranch house.

By this time four of Cameron's hands and all of Cameron's children were following alongside in a ragged circle. Soon they were joined by Cameron's wife—a woman, Longarm remembered, that Annabelle had referred to as no more than a steady, dependable beast of burden. She looked like nothing of the kind. Her eyes were large and gentle, her sensitive, pretty face suffused with concern for the injured girl. And judging from the way everyone made way for her as she approached, Longarm could see at once what a source of warmth she was, not only for her brood of children, but for her husband and his ranch hands as well.

"We were bushwhacked by one of Roland Smith's teamsters," Longarm said, in answer to Cameron's question. "His first shot got Annabelle's horse, and when she came down, she struck her head on a rock."

"Oh dear," said Cameron's wife. "That could be very serious. Carry her right on in and put her down on my bed."

As she spoke, Cameron's wife led the way to her bedroom. The moment Longarm put Annabelle down on the bed, Cameron's wife waved everyone from the room so she could tend to Annabelle.

Cameron shooed his kids from the house, dismissed his men, and proceeded to make some coffee for Longarm, who slumped wearily down into a chair at the kitchen table. The two men had already introduced themselves, and Longarm had described how he and Frank Fools Crow had released Annabelle the day before from Radley's makeshift stockade.

He shook his head in dismay. "That girl sure has suffered some, and that's a fact. First the Radleys and now this fall. But don't you worry none about Annabelle," Cameron told Longarm. "Faith'll take good care of her." He shook his head in admiration. "She's a wonder with anyone sick— animals or people, it don't matter which."

He poured both himself and Longarm a mug of coffee, then sat down opposite the lawman. "Now," he said. "You got any idea why in tarnation one of Smitty's teamsters would be after you?"

"Someone paid him."

"Paid him?"

"That's right."

"You got any idea why?"

"Nope." Longarm sipped the hot coffee.

"Which teamster was it?"

"I don't know his name. He didn't introduce himself to me before he commenced shooting. He looked like a pirate, though. Had a red bandanna wrapped around his head and wore a green eye patch."

Cameron nodded. "That'd be Hale Murdock. If you bested that man, mister, you did yourself proud. Even Smitty—as big as he is—would think twice before tangling with that snake. Not that Murdock was a big man. No, sir. That wasn't what bothered a man about Murdock. He was just an example of pure meanness, clear through to the marrow in his bones." Cameron took a sip of his coffee and leaned closer. "And you're *sure* someone hired him to kill you?"

"That's what I said."

"What makes you so sure? A man like Murdock didn't

really need much of an excuse, and if you're up here to back the play of the revenuers, you got to expect this kind of thing, just on general principles."

"Maybe." Then Longarm told him about the two hundred in freshly minted gold coins he had found in Murdock's saddlebag.

Cameron nodded. "Got any idea who would hire Murdock to kill you?"

"Maybe the murderer of those four revenuers, the ones that were found south of here all mutilated—not those last two that Lester Radley killed."

Cameron frowned. "What's that? Which two men are you talking about?"

"A couple of Treasury agents the Radleys were using to help harvest their crop. They got away, but it seems Lester Radley caught up with them. Me and Annabelle found their corpses in Beaver Pass."

Cameron shook his head. "This is sure nasty business, all right." The man looked warily at Longarm, then took a deep breath. "All right. Maybe you better tell me now. Why have you come here to my ranch, Deputy?"

"I need help. The Radleys and the MacLaggans are probably after me right now for helping Frank Fools Crow free his brother and sister—and for freeing Annabelle, as well."

Longarm thought he saw Cameron blush slightly at mention of Annabelle's name, but the rancher covered up nicely.

"Those devils," Cameron muttered angrily. "But that's the kind of animals the Radleys are, using people as if they were slaves."

"And I've already told you about that grizzly that Frank Fools Crow set on them. Looks to me like they took a fearful mauling. So the Radleys and the MacLaggans should be prowling this high country right now, looking for my scalp along with Frank Fools Crow."

Cameron nodded gloomily. "Well, you can count on my help, Long."

"I know that, and I thank you, Cameron. But are there any other settlers in these parts who might be willing to back my play?"

Cameron shook his head warily. "Well now, Marshal,

there's sure enough settlers and ranchers around here who don't much like them buzzards. But few of them would relish getting on the wrong side of them. They'd sooner sleep in a nest of scorpions, I'm thinking."

Longarm looked at Cameron closely. The owner of the Bar C had impressed him from the first. He was a smooth-shaven fellow with gleaming dark eyes that looked with solid, uncompromising honesty out at the world. He was at least six feet tall and there was not an ounce of unwanted tallow on his spare frame. One glance at his tanned features and heavily callused hands told Longarm that here was a rancher who was not above pitching in beside his hired men.

"And do you include yourself among them, Cameron?" Longarm asked.

"Hell, yes," the man said, grinning suddenly. "And, I might add, I count myself a frequent purchaser of their product, as well. It's the finest hooch this side of the Mississippi."

"Then you won't help me."

"Didn't say that. Said we'd sooner sleep in a nest of scorpions. Of course I'll help you. And I'll do what I can to rope in my neighbors. Just don't expect us to do it too cheerful, that's all."

"I don't care about your enthusiasm," Longarm told him. "Just give me the help I'll need."

"How do you mean to move on them?"

"Hit them at their most vulnerable point. They've been making mincemeat of the Treasury men Washington has been sending out here. So we'll do what we can to finish what those poor souls started."

"Destroy their stills."

"That's right. *And* their barley crop, what they've managed to store already."

"That's a tall order."

"I know it."

"In fact, you're suggesting a revolution. You'll be taking away their livelihood. Such a move will not only affect the MacLaggans and the Radleys, but Smitty and his crew of teamsters, as well."

"Why them?"

"Hell, Long, who in tarnation do you think delivers that scamper juice to market?"

Longarm frowned. Of course. He should have realized it. The MacLaggans and Radleys were the moonshiners, but it was Smitty and his teamsters who were bootlegging the white lightning. A perfect setup. Smitty hauled the U.S. Mail north, and MacLaggan's mountain dew south.

Longarm shrugged. "In that case, maybe it *would* be asking too much to expect you to go against that crowd."

Cameron held up his hand. "Now hold it just a minute, Long. Them federal agents ain't the only gents them Radleys have taken after in years past. There ain't a one of us who hasn't felt the lash of their lawlessness. Them MacLaggans and Radleys think they own these mountains. And if they keep on the way they been going, they damn well might end up doing just that." He nodded his head shortly, decisively. "I'm thinking maybe you happened along at just the right time, Long. Seems to me that now's when we should throw in with you and declare our independence."

He strode to the door and flung it open. "Pete! Bo! Will! Get in here!"

He turned back to Longarm. "I'll send my men out tonight. We should have ourselves a fine war party gathered in this here kitchen by this time tomorrow. Then we can make our plans. How's that suit you?"

Longarm nodded emphatically. That suited him just fine.

Chapter 7

Earlier that same afternoon, Dudley Withers had heard Hale
Murdock open fire on Longarm. He was less than a mile
from the ridge, and pulled up the moment he caught the
sound of gunfire. As soon as he was sure where the firing
was coming from, he let loose with a dark stream of tobacco
juice and clapped spurs to his horse.

Dudley was the only one besides Radley and his two
remaining sons to have escaped the fury of Frank Fools
Crow's grizzly, and while Radley and Ma tended to Miles
Farnum, Dudley had decided it would clear his head some
if he started his own search for that damned half-breed.
Now, filled with a sudden grim hope, he drove his horse
without mercy over the rocky, treacherous ground. Hell,
maybe someone—one of the MacLaggans, possibly—had
cornered the Indian.

The firing ceased, however, before Dudley reached the
base of the ridge, but he kept on nevertheless, driving his
mount mercilessly. At the very last, when he found the high
ground too difficult to negotiate on horseback, he flung
himself from his horse, yanked his rifle from its sling, and

angled swiftly up the slope toward the rimrock above.

What he found when he reached the ridge were spent casings from a Winchester—and all around them on the ground what looked like the mark of a fierce struggle. He followed the bootprints around a huge boulder to a smooth section of caprock. Crouching to keep himself from slipping on the treacherous gravel, he looked closer and saw a long, ragged streak of dried blood on the rock—and, wedged in a niche in the rock farther down, what appeared to be the remains of a man's hand. Flies swarmed over it and white bone gleamed in the sun. Dudley studied it for a moment, swallowed, then turned away. He found a ledge from which he could look down at the foot of the escarpment, and climbed carefully out onto it. Below the caprock, crumpled on the talus at the foot of the slope, he saw the still, broken body of Hale Murdock. He recognized the man from the red bandanna still wrapped about his head.

Looking beyond into the valley then, he made out two riders, their mounts belly-deep in grass as they moved across the lush parkland. One of them, a woman in a ragged dress, appeared to be wounded, judging from the way she rode. The two riders were heading northwest to the pine flats beyond—to the Bar C, more than likely. Narrowing his eyes, Dudley peered carefully at the riders and thought the wounded girl might possibly be that whore, Annabelle. The other was a big man and rode tall enough in the saddle to be that deputy marshal—the one Ma said was in cahoots with the breed.

So that was two of them. The half-breed sure as hell couldn't be far, then. And they were heading for Cameron's Bar C, were they? Dudley had never liked Cameron. Without making a show if it, the man was too damned decent. Hell, he was an honest man. And what the hell could you do with that kind of man? No matter how much Radley had offered him, Cameron had refused to throw in with them and put some of this lush valley of his into barley.

Dudley spat a long, dark stream of tobacco juice over the tip of the ledge, stood up, and made his way back to the ridge. He'd found two of them, anyway, and he knew where to gather them in when the time came. Now he'd get back and see how Miles Farnum was doing—not that the poor son of a bitch stood much of a chance, with half his goddamn back peeled off like an onion skin.

It was dusk when Dudley rode in. Simpson Radley was in the doorway to the farmhouse, his two remaining boys beside him. Jed and Dan. They were only twenty and twenty-two, and they lacked the meanness of Lester and the fun-loving deviltry of poor Lafe, but they were all Rad had left, and he'd have to make do.

Dudley dismounted and gave the reins of his mount to Pa Radley. As Pa led Dudley's horse over to the barn, Ma Radley appeared in the doorway behind her son.

"Where the hell you been?" Rad asked.

"Been doin' some hunting," said Dudley. "I was hoping I might cut that damn breed's sign. I went back to his cabin. He done burned it down."

Dudley started toward the farmhouse.

"There's some bodies there we got to take care of."

"I know that, dammit," said Rad. "Is that all you found?"

Dudley smiled. He was a wide, blocky fellow with short, chubby legs and arms, a round, tough face, and eyes as flat and lusterless as old coins. He wore a black, floppy-brimmed hat, a soiled red-checked shirt, and Levi's that needed washing. The only thing really clean and bright about him was the Colt on his hip.

He stuffed a thick wad of chewing tobacco past his tobacco-stained teeth and smiled. "I found that whore and the deputy marshal. Looks like one of Smitty's men did too. Only he came out on the short end."

"Stop speakin' in riddles," Ma said, pushing past Rad. "What're you tellin' us?"

"I didn't see what happened. But what I know for sure is that Hale Murdock is dead and it's that deputy marshal what killed him."

"Did you see that deputy?" Ma asked.

Dudley nodded and sent a long brown arrow of tobacco juice from the corner of his mouth. "I saw them riding through the valley, heading toward the Bar C. Looks like that's where they'll hole up for a while. The whore was shot, looked like. 'Course, I couldn't be sure. And I may be wrong about them heading for Cameron's ranch, too."

"Dammit!" cried Simpson Radley. "You gonna tell us what happened?"

But Dudley would not be rushed. He was enjoying himself too much. "I reckon it was Hale tried to bushwhack the deputy from the ridge on the other side of Beaver Pass, but he missed his chance and the deputy took after him. That's the way it looks to me, because right now Murdock's body is lying at the foot of the ridge, with his right hand shot off."

Ma looked at her son in surprise. "Now why in hell would Smitty send one of his men after the deputy?"

"Now how the hell would I know that, Ma?" Rad asked wearily.

"Well," she said, her eyes gleaming in satisfaction, "we'll take all the help we can get. And that reminds me— we ought to send someone into Red Gap. We could use some of Smitty's men."

"I'll go," said Dudley wearily. "After I get some grub, if you don't mind. How's Miles?"

"He's gone," she said grimly, looking suddenly away and up at the hills beyond the farm, where the family burial plot was located. "We'll be burying him soon, I'm thinking. Then . . . we'll go after Lafe's body."

Rad nodded. He had expected Farnum's death, but now he didn't know what to say. All he felt himself was relief that Miles was out of his misery. With half his back torn out, he had been in constant pain. Once, Dudley had suggested to Ma that maybe it would be a good idea if they let him put a bullet through the man's brain. But Simpson would have none of it.

Rad and Miles had been friends since they were kids. They'd come west together and were closer than brothers. Now, looking at the bleak emptiness in Rad's eyes, he wondered how the man could stand up under what had happened to him these past weeks.

And most of this because they'd tangled with that halfbreed. Dudley shook his head. It was so goddamn hard to believe.

"The MacLaggans'll be here soon," Rad reminded Dudley, "to help with this crop. Then we'll make a visit to the Bar C. I been waiting for Cameron to stick his nose in. This is all the excuse I'll need." Rad looked closely at Dudley. "That breed. Any sign of him?"

Dudley shook his head. "But him and that deputy are in cahoots, so he won't be far. Don't worry. We'll catch the son of a bitch."

"Come inside," said Ma. "There's fresh coffee on."

Pa, returning from the barn, sang out, "That's for me! A little moonshine and coffee."

They acted as if they hadn't heard the old man as they crowded into the farmhouse. The moment Dudley stepped through the door, he smelled the body of Miles Farnum as it lay in the bedroom. The hand of corruption had already begun to probe its dead flesh. As Dudley slumped into a chair at the kitchen table, he wondered if he would be able to keep the coffee down.

Pa was right. What they all needed now was coffee *and* moonshine. And after that, he prayed to God, they would bury the poor dead son of a bitch.

Cal Hardman of the Box H rode into the Bar C along with his three boys about sundown the following day. Right behind him came Matt Stokes of the Lazy S. He had brought with him his foreman and his grandfather. Not far behind them, riding in a handsome buggy they had recently purchased from Montgomery Ward, came Seth Robinson and his wife Clara.

He was the only granger Cameron had invited to the meeting. A God-fearing, Bible-thumping preacher, he had long been outraged by the arrogant trespasses of the Radleys and MacLaggans. He was a gaunt, broad-shouldered giant of a man, with a massive beard, and eyes that gleamed with a fiery intensity. As he pulled up in his buggy, the others all waited for him to help his wife down. They tipped their hats to her, then let the woman lead the way into the Cameron ranch house, where Faith Cameron was waiting to greet them.

When she was not tending to Annabelle, Faith had been

91

preparing all day for the meeting. She had put enough coffee on to float an ironclad, and had baked plates of doughnuts and cakes. The kitchen was filled with the smell of her cooking. Now, wearing a fresh gingham dress, her long hair combed out, she waited with her daughter at her side and greeted Clara Robinson and her husband, then the others in turn.

Cameron introduced each one to Longarm separately, then they found places around the deal table that Cameron had brought out into the big main living room. There was a fire crackling in the huge fireplace, since this night, like almost every night in this high country, had already turned chill. The coffee and doughnuts were passed around first, and Longarm let each party get reacquainted. He was well aware of how seldom they had this kind of a chance to catch up.

Matt Stokes's grandfather did not sit at the table. He preferred a stool in the corner and contented himself with a jug of white lightning he had brought with him. He sat there with impressive dignity and watched the proceedings with bright, alert eyes, the mouth of his jug never too far from his lips. Clara Robinson helped Faith serve the men, then discreetly vanished into the bedroom with Faith to visit with the still-ailing Annabelle.

Cameron called the meeting to order by going to the door and calling out to his hired men, Pete, Bo, and Will. As soon as these three tramped in, his three boys following after, Cameron sat down at the head of the table, with Longarm by his side, and tapped a spoon on the side of his coffee mug. The room quieted.

"This here's Deputy U.S. Marshal Long," Cameron said. "He's come here to do something about the moonshiners, and he needs our help. Like I told him yesterday, there ain't been one of us who hasn't felt the lash of their lawlessness. So what I told him was that maybe now's the right time for us to stand up to those buzzards—with the deputy's help. But I'll let him tell you. That's why I sent for you." Cameron turned to Longarm. "Go ahead, Long. You got the floor."

The room grew silent as every eye turned to Longarm.

He cleared his throat. "I'm here," he said, "because of the murder of six U.S. Government employees. Revenue men. Four of them were not killed very quickly; they were dumped in the Snake River and washed up near Taylor's Ferry."

"Revenuers!" snorted the old man sitting in the corner. "They ought to go find honest work! Good whiskey's hard to make, and them MacLaggans brew the best damn whiskey ever tickled my tonsils."

Matt Stokes turned to regard his grandfather. "Gramps," he said, "you just sit there and enjoy that brew. Otherwise, come up here to this table and take your lumps. This deputy ain't talkin' about moonshine, he's talkin' about murder."

"I know what he's talkin' about," grumbled the old man. "But they wouldn't be no murders if the government'd keep its nose out of decent people's business!"

"Since when," boomed Seth Robinson, his eyes suddenly alight with indignation, "do we call the MacLaggans and Radleys *decent* people!"

"Aw, the hell with it," said Gramps, returning to his jug. "I ain't gonna argue with God."

Cal Hardman said mildly, "All right, Seth. We'll agree that the Radleys and the MacLaggans don't go to church on Sunday, but Gramps has got a point. Making our own whiskey shouldn't be a crime, and them government agents could do a whole lot better by going after renegade Indians—or the cattle thieves and highwaymen that infest the West, and make it unsafe for decent people to go abroad."

There was general murmur of agreement to this. Longarm waited patiently for it to die down. When it did, he spoke again.

"I tend to agree with you gents," he said reasonably. "And I'm the man the government usually sends out to pick up those highwaymen and cattle thieves you complain about. But at the moment—as Matt just pointed out—I'm interested in murderers, not rustlers or moonshiners. But the way it looks to me, there is a very good chance that those doing the moonshining are also responsible for them murders. It don't make no never-mind to me that these here

93

revenuers are on a fool's errand. I'll grant you that. But they worked for the U.S. Government, same as I do, and they were murdered."

Cameron spoke up then. "Long has already killed Lester Radley. And Lester is the one he believes killed two revenue agents he just found in Beaver Pass. But he still don't have the ones responsible for killing and mutilating those four agents that were found near Taylor's Ferry."

"Why, hell, Deputy," said Cal Hardman. "Sure you do! If Lester Radley killed them two you just found, he killed then other ones too. You don't need us."

There was quick agreement to that, from everyone but Cameron. Seth Robinson's voice was the loudest of all. When he had finished voicing his agreement with Cal's sentiments, he leaned back in his chair and regarded Longarm with cold, accusing eyes. It was obvious what he was thinking: Why in tarnation had Longarm dragged them out for this meeting if he had already found and killed the murderer?

Calmly, Longarm said, "I disagree. I don't think Lester Radley killed those four Treasury men."

"Maybe you better spell that out, Deputy," said Cal Hardman, his voice sharp with impatience. His three boys, each one as grim about the mouth as their father, leaned forward with him to listen.

"Lester Radley killed the two revenuers I found, just the way he would have killed me, if he had the chance. In cold blood, without even blinking. Then, just as he would have done with me, he buried the bodies where he killed them. There's no telling how many Treasury agents have fertilized the rocky hills and hollows of my own home state, nor how many the Radleys have planted over the years in this high country. But no one will ever know, because they never got found. And that's the way the Radleys and the MacLaggans operate. They use the earth to cover their crimes. They don't advertise their killings."

"Your point, Deputy?" Matt said.

"My point is just this. Neither Lester Radley nor any of his clan killed the revenuers that got washed up near Taylor's Ferry. I allow they were last seen in Red Gap, moving into

94

these mountains. But if Lester had killed them, he would have buried them. He wouldn't have bothered to cut them up and then gone to the trouble of making sure they were discovered near Taylor's Ferry."

"You say they were mutilated?" asked Matt Stokes.

Longarm nodded.

"Then, if the Radleys or the MacLaggans didn't do it, I'd say Indians done it. Renegades. Like that half-breed, Frank Fools Crow."

"I don't think so."

"Why, sure! If they was cut up, it was Indians done it," said Gramps, wiping his wrinkled mouth with the back of his bony wrist. "Yessir!" he cried, his voice rising as he warmed to his topic. "Them savages like nothin' better than to see a while man squirm. They ought to send in the army, that's what. Clear out these mountains. They got more renegade Sioux and Cheyenne in 'em than a dog has fleas!"

Matt looked at Longarm, his face impassive, his mind obviously made up. "Gramps has got a point, Deputy. If it ain't the Radleys done it, I'd say go look for them renegade Indians."

"Frank Fools Crow!" said Seth Robinson. "He's the one!"

"You're sure of that, are you?" asked Longarm. "He saved my life after Lester Radley near killed me. I don't reckon he would have killed them revenuers. What would be his motive?"

"Hell!" cried Cal Hardman, slapping the table forcefully. "Who says them heathens need a motive! They kill for the pure dumb pleasure of it! I don't much care what he done for you, Deputy. That half-breed is as capable of killing a revenue agent as any moonshiner is."

Seth Robinson spoke up then, his voice cold. "Just what was it you wanted from us, Deputy?"

"I would like to deputize you. Then we could round up the Radleys and the MacLaggans, put an end to their moonshining in these parts. There's a good chance that once we got them on the run, they would cough up whoever it was murdered them revenuers."

"You already said you didn't think the Radleys did it."

"I know that. But unless one of you did it, then it has to be them—or someone in cahoots with them."

"And of course Frank Fools Crow could not possibly have done it," Robinson said.

"I do not think so."

Matt's foreman spoke up then. His voice was surprisingly soft, almost gentle. "I was in Red Gap this morning. Dudley Withers rode in looking for Smitty and his teamsters. He said Lafe Radley and three other Radley men were killed by a grizzly that Frank Fools Crow set on them."

There was a shocked silence, then all eyes turned to Longarm. Longarm nodded. "I know. I was there. The grizzly was a ruse to keep the Radleys occupied while we freed the folks that the Radleys had pressed into service as hired hands. Frank Fools Crow had no notion that the grizzly would do so much damage. And neither did I."

"You see!" cried Seth Robinson triumphantly. "That Indian is in league with the devil! He can make the wild beasts of the forest act on his behalf! I tell you, Deputy, *he's* your man!" He looked triumphantly around him. "Furthermore, gentlemen, I have a surprise for you—and for this naive deputy marshal, as well."

"Let's have it, Seth," said Matt wearily.

"I have already captured the Sioux half-breed. Frank Fools Crow was taken by my men only hours before I set out for this meeting. At present he is being held in my horse barn. I have chained him to one of the stanchions."

The news was a sensation. Everyone tried to talk at once. But it was Cameron who hushed them with his hand and looked to Longarm, awaiting his response.

"Why did you do that?" Longarm asked. "What had Frank Fools Crow done?"

"He was riding across my land. He is an Indian. Like all the rest of them, he should be in a government agency. I am sick of seeing heathen run loose, so soon after that treacherous massacre of the Seventh Cavalry—and the man who might have been our next President!"

"You mean Custer."

"Precisely."

96

"A hell of a President he would have made," snorted Cal Hardman.

"That's beside the point," said Matt. "Seth's right. Them Indians ain't got no right to ride around like they still own this land. After what they done, the only home they got is up there in Canada with Sittin' Bull, or in a government agency. And that's a fact."

Cal looked at Longarm. "There's your murderer, Deputy. Seth here has caught him for you. All you have to do is ride back with him and pick him up. You can deliver him to Colonel Walthers on your way out of here. I'm sure the colonel will know what to do with him."

"I see," drawled Longarm. "Frank Fools Crow did it. He murdered and mutilated four revenue agents, all by himself."

"No," said Seth Robinson. "He had help. The devil was at his side—or perhaps another grizzly!"

Longarm expected that statement to be greeted with derision; instead, a sudden, hushed silence fell over the men. To Longarm's dismay, he realized that in their present mood, these men before him were quite willing—even anxious—to believe what Seth Robinson had just suggested to them: that Frank Fools Crow, in league with the devil, had killed those four revenuers.

Seth Robinson got to his feet. "I think this meeting is over, gentlemen. We do not need to ride against our neighbors, the Radleys and the MacLaggans. The culprit Deputy Long is seeking has already been captured. Will you take delivery now, Deputy?"

"I'll take Frank Fools Crow off your hands, yes," said Longarm.

"And you'll deliver the breed to justice."

"That I will," said Longarm grimly.

"Fine!" boomed Seth. "Then I would say that we have all accomplished a good night's work."

After that triumphant pronouncement, it did not take long for the men to leave. They fairly flew out the door. Robinson almost dragged his wife out of the bedroom, where she was visiting with Faith and Annabelle, and in less than five minutes the hoofbeats of the departing guests were fading fast.

Standing in the cabin doorway beside Longarm, Cameron shook his head in disgust. "Seems like they were willing to believe anything, if only they didn't have to tangle with the MacLaggans or Radleys. I guess they won't be much help, Long."

"Don't let it get you down. It wasn't exactly fair of me to ask them for help anyway. Hell, this is my job. It's what I'm gettin' paid to do, don't forget."

"What are you going to do now?"

"I'm going in there and say goodbye to Annabelle. Then I'm going to overtake Seth Robinson. He's got a friend of mine in chains, don't forget."

"I won't ask you what you intend to do."

"Good."

"Longarm," Annabelle said, sitting up quickly as Longarm closed the door softly, then sat down on the edge of her bed. "Where are you going at this hour?"

"To help a friend."

"What do you mean?"

"It's a long story. I'll tell you when I get back."

"Oh, you must take me away from here. Promise me you will."

"You don't like it here?"

"It's . . . it's not that. Oh, you know why I must not stay here, Longarm."

"Yes," he said, smiling. "I guess I do."

She sighed deeply. "You have no idea, Longarm," she said, "how humble I feel."

He put his hat down on the bed and took her hand in his. "Well now, what brought that on?"

"Faith. She . . . she's so good and kind. And Harley had made me think she was such a drudge. How *could* he be unfaithful to her, Longarm? Oh, it makes me feel so awful."

"You said 'humble' before," he reminded her gently.

"I feel humble when she tends to me, and I see how she is with her children and how hard she works. She is so good! And then I see Harley and hear his voice—and sometimes, when he looks at me—I feel awful."

"Because you love him."

"Yes!"

He patted her hand, then leaned over and kissed her on the forehead. "I'll come back for you. Don't you worry. How's your head?"

"I'm still dizzy when I stand up, and I've still got a headache. But it's better now. I don't see spots anymore." She smiled. "And my, it's good to see you. Do hurry back, Longarm."

He put on his hat and stood up. "I will. And that's a promise."

He left the bedroom, said his goodbyes to Harley and his wife, and rode out after Seth Robinson. The moon was bright and the trail not difficult to follow. Cameron had given him directions to the Robinson farm, so that Longarm felt quite confident he would have no difficulty finding it, even if he was not able to overtake the man.

Now, as he rode through the moonlit night, he found himself recalling once again how eager those men had been to believe anything at all, if only it gave them the excuse they needed not to take action. He shook his head. He knew he should not blame them. And he should not feel comtempt for them, either.

But he did.

Chapter 8

Longarm found Frank Fools Crow standing in chains, defiant.

Seth Robinson had been waiting for Longarm in the barn. But as Longarm strode in and came to a halt in front of him, the man made no effort to unchain the half-breed. Instead, flanked by his two hired hands and one eighteen-year-old son, he rocked back on his heels and said, "I want your word, Deputy, that you'll see to it that this heathen is brought to justice. To a God-fearing, white man's justice."

"You mean Colonel Walthers."

"The colonel is a man who understands how to deal with these heathen, yes."

"I'll have to see about that. What was this Indian's crime?"

"Trespassin'!" Robinson's boy said, speaking up suddenly, his eyes narrowing as he plowed a lock of flaxen hair back off his forehead. "Trespassin' on our land. He said he was going to build himself a cabin, that this was his father's place many years ago."

"That's not so unlikely," Longarm replied. "His father

was a white man who lived in these parts at one time, before your father and the other settlers found this high valley."

"Just as I thought," Seth Robinson said. "You're taking his side, aren't you, Deputy?"

As he spoke, his boy and the two hired hands moved closer with menacing suddenness. One of the hired hands, a fat fellow with yellow suspenders and a round, doughlike face, lifted a pitchfork—his only weapon, apparently.

With a sigh, Longarm unlimbered his Colt and leveled it at Seth. "Tell your boy to free the Indian, Seth. You have no right to imprison this man. He has done you no harm. If you don't want him to build a cabin on your land, he'll find some other place." Longarm looked at Fools Crow. "Ain't that right, Frank?"

Fools Crow nodded slightly, reluctantly.

"Do as I say," Longarm repeated. "Free this man. Now."

Seth Robinson studied the lawman's face, then the revolver in his hand. Reluctantly he said, "You heard this Indian-lover, son. Do as he says."

Longarm stepped back as the boy moved closer to Fools Crow and unlocked the padlocks that held the chains imprisoning Frank Fools Crow. In a moment the Indian stepped clear and, with impressive dignity, took his place beside Longarm.

Too late, Longarm heard the sound of a light footfall in the hay behind him. He started to turn as something crashed down upon his head with an odd metallic clang. He was unconscious before he hit the floor.

Less than an hour before, Simpson Radley, peering down at the Bar C ranch, shifted in his saddle to look at Dennis MacLaggan, his face hard, his eyes blazing with suppressed fury.

"There they go! The whole damn pack of them! They've thrown in with that deputy and the Indian. It's them or us now!"

MacLaggan frowned and continued to peer down at Harley Cameron's ranch house. Behind them waited six more riders: his own two sons; Rad's two sons; MacLaggan's blacksmith, Ed Stoner; and Dudley Withers.

"I told you," said Dudley. "I knew that deputy was headin' this way."

MacLaggan turned to Rad. "We don't know if that deputy has had any part in this, Rad. You're just guessin'. There's no real proof that Cameron—or any of those men we just saw leave—have thrown in with the deputy. You heard what Dudley said. The Svenson woman was wounded, and the nearest help they could find was at this ranch. So naturally, the deputy headed this way."

"You gettin' silly in your old age, Dennis?" Rad demanded. "You saw them riders. You saw who they were. There was a meeting in that ranch house tonight. And I'm bettin' that deputy ran it. You know how these ranchers and that crazy Bible-thumper see us. They'll drink our liquor, but they wouldn't give us the time of day. And Seth Robinson would sooner cross the street than greet me civilly— even when I offered to buy some of his damned snake oil."

"I think maybe he thinks he's in competition with us," Dudley said, chuckling. "If'n you ever tasted any of that elixir of his, you'd know why."

Dennis ignored Dudley's remark. "So what do you plan to do, Rad?"

"Why, I'll just ride on down there and ask Cameron where that deputy is and where that Indian might be hiding."

"And if he don't know?"

Rad smiled. "He knows, Dennis. Don't you worry. He's working *with* that deputy!"

"Hey, look!" said Tim, his voice hushed with excitement. "Ain't that the deputy ridin' out now?"

Rad turned quickly around in his saddle, his face alight with triumph as he saw the tall figure astride the horse below him, moving already at a full gallop as he left Cameron's yard. "It sure as hell is," said Rad exultantly.

"He looks like he's trying to catch up to the rest," said Dudley.

Rad turned back to Dennis. "You still want to argue, Dennis?"

"Guess maybe you called it at that, Rad," he agreed reluctantly.

"Go after him, Dennis. Take whoever you think you

eed. I'm thinkin' he just might lead you to that Indu.... I'll stay here and settle up with Cameron."

"All right," said MacLaggan. "But go easy on the poor son of a bitch, will you? He probably don't know nothing about the trouble that deputy and the half-breed caused you."

"Sure," said Rad. "I'll go easy on the bastard."

MacLaggan pointed to his two sons and Ed Stoner, then spurred his horse off the ridge after the deputy.

Rad waited until the four of them had disappeared in the darkness, than angled his horse cautiously down the slope, with Dudley and his own two boys following after.

Annabelle sat up. That loud pounding on the cabin door could only mean trouble. A chill ran up her spine. Then she heard the tiny, startled cry of dismay from Faith as the sound of heavy boots suddenly filled the cabin.

She threw back her covers and ran to the bedroom door, ignoring the sudden dizziness that almost caused her to crash into the wall. The door was slightly ajar. Peering out, she caught a glimpse of Simpson Radley's round, piggish face and long, scraggly beard—and behind him, his two sons. They were crowding into the cabin, their guns drawn!

She could not see Harley, but she could hear his angry voice as he demanded what Radley and his gang meant by storming into his cabin in this fashion. Radley's voice answered harshly, and then she heard heavy steps approaching the bedroom. Before she could duck back, the door was flung open and Dudley Withers was standing before her, a huge revolver in his hand, a mean grin on his face.

"Here's the slut," he called back over his shoulder to Radley.

Before she knew what she was doing, Annabelle reached out and slapped Dudley in the face. The man's head barely moved as it absorbed the blow. The mean smile still on his face, he brought the Colt around with a vicious swipe and caught her on the side of the jaw.

Lights exploded deep inside her skull, and the next thing she knew she had slammed to the floor, the side of her head coming to rest sharply against the doorjamb. She tried to speak out, to show her rage at this treatment, but she could not speak. Something was wrong with her jaw. She reached up and took hold of it. The moment she did, a blinding pain erupted behind it. Uttering a strangled cry of pain, she slumped forward onto the floor.

Dudley stepped back, then carefully kicked her in the side. She hung on to consciousness only by a thread as she rolled over from the force of the blow and saw Harley, in four rapid strides, overtake Dudley from the rear and spin him around. Harley was weaponless, but his right fist shot out and caught Dudley in the midsection. Dudley buckled, gasping. Again Harley struck out at Dudley, catching him this time on the side of the head.

Staggering back, Dudley remained on his feet, brought up his revolver, and fired point-blank at Harley. She watched in horror as Harley, struck in the stomach, staggered back. She heard Faith's agonized scream and saw her rush to Harley's side. Radley rushed over after her and flung Faith back away from her husband. When she tried to return to him, he slapped her sharply, grabbed her, and flung her back into the corner where her four children were cowering.

Harley managed somehow to stay on his feet.

"Where's that Indian, Harley?" Radley asked the wounded man. "You better tell me where he is or I'll string your kids up, one by one!"

As wounded as he was, Harley reached out with a bloody hand and tried to clasp Radley about the neck. But Radley stepped back, took out his own weapon, and cocked it.

"I mean it, you stupid son of a bitch! I'll finish you right now! Where's that Indian? We saw that deputy marshal leave here. Now tell us!"

"I . . . I don't know," Harley gasped, slipping slowly forward onto his knees, a widening pool of blood growing on the floor beneath him. He was holding his abdomen with both hands now, but the blood was streaming through his fingers in a steady, pulsing flow.

Annabelle knew where the Indian was. He was at Seth Robinson's farm! But when she tried to move her jaw to speak, it sent another excruciating dagger of pain up through kull, and all she could manage was a painful groan. Tears from the pain sprang into her eyes.

It was Faith who told Radley.

"The Indian's at Seth Robinson's farm!" she cried out. "Leave Harley be, Mr. Radley! Please!"

Radley straightened and holstered his weapon. With a smile, he looked at Dudley and his two sons. Then he looked across the room at Faith. "And that deputy marshal has gone to him. Ain't that right?"

"Yes!"

"Well, that's all I came for. MacLaggan'll have it all wrapped up nice and tidy by the time we get there, sure enough."

Then, in a burst of exuberant malice, he walked over to the kitchen table, picked up the kerosene lantern, and flung it at the wall beside the bedroom doorway. In an instant the splattered kerosene covered the wall with flame. There was another lamp near the fireplace. Radley reached that as quickly as he had the other, and flung it the length of the cabin. It hit the far wall and, with a deep *whump*, sent flames spilling up the wall and across the ceiling.

Annabelle flung herself away from the bedroom doorway as the flames spread with incredible swiftness. Radley, almost hidden by the black smoke pulsing from the two flaming walls, herded his two sons out of the cabin ahead of him, Dudley following hard on his heels.

Ignoring the awful pain in her jaw, Annabelle hastened to Harley's side, as did the man's wife. Together the two women managed to drag him to the door, the children hurrying out of the cabin ahead of them. Even as Annabelle pulled Harley into the cool night, she saw that the two barns were also on fire and heard the sound of repeated gunfire as Pete, Bo, and Will—well hidden in the darkness—fired back at Radley and his riders. The night was filled with the awesome, hellish glow from the leaping flames and the angry whine of ricocheting bullets. Annabelle glanced up as Radley and his men galloped out of the yard, yipping like animals and firing back with random fury at the flaming barns and cabin.

A bullet struck the ground just in front of Annabelle. She

ducked her head away—and into the path of a second bullet, which crashed into her left temple, killing her instantly.

Longarm regained consciousness in Seth Robinson's new buggy. Clara and Seth were on the front seat, Seth driving their high-stepping team of blacks through the night with an astonishing recklessness. It was the sharp crack of his whip that had brought Longarm around.

Longarm's hands were tied cruelly behind him. His hat was crushed under him and his Colt was missing, but he could feel his derringer resting still in his right vest pocket. Beside him, sitting up in the back seat, his hands also tied behind him, was Frank Fools Crow.

In the darkness, Longarm thought he saw the Indian smile.

"Where the hell are we going?" Longarm asked the Indian, his voice barely audible above the pounding of the horses' hooves and the rumbling of the wagon's iron-rimmed wheels.

It was Clara who answered. She turned to look down at him. "You try anything, mister," she told him, "and I'll give you another whack with this frying pan!"

As she spoke, she waved it threateningly at him. Longarm winced and pulled away from her just as the wagon bucked and went airborne as it flew over a boulder in the road. The woman pulled quickly back around and, in her anxiety to find something to hang on to, nearly lost her weapon.

Longarm swore unhappily. Caught from behind by a woman with a frying pan! If he lived through this, he hoped Billy Vail never found out about it. Now he knew why Frank Fools Crow was smiling.

"You might tell me where we're going in such an all-fired hurry, ma'am," Longarm called to the woman. "It's mighty uncomfortable back here."

"It'll be a darn sight less comfortable where you're going," snapped the woman.

Frank Fools Crow spoke up then. "They ride into the hills to find place where they can kill us."

"Kill us?"

"Yes Longarm. And bury us."

"You're crazy, Fools Crow!" Longarm protested.

"No. I am not crazy. This preacher and his woman— *they* are crazy. You will see."

Longarm could not believe what Fools Crow was saying. This Bible-thumping prophet of the Lord and his wife were an odd enough pair, all right—but one of them was a preacher! Fools Crow had obviously misunderstood their intentions.

"Ma'am!" Longarm called out above the earsplitting rattle of the buggy. "I'm a federal officer. I demand you untie me and Fools Crow!"

"Oh, we couldn't do that," the woman told Longarm over her shoulder. "Not now. Not after we have assaulted you. We have committed a criminal offense. We know that. The only thing for us to do now is get rid of the evidence of our crime."

"I promise you! I won't press charges!"

But Seth Robinson and his wife were no longer listening.

A moment later, Robinson pulled off the road and drove the buggy through a moonlit grove of aspen. "Here we are!" he said, as he left the grove and reined in the horses.

As the buggy rattled to a stop, Longarm managed to lift his head enough to glance out through the side curtains and see that they were on the slope of a hill overlooking the valley. And above them, at the very crest of the hill, outlined in the pale moonlight, were at least a dozen headstones.

These two lunatics were serious!

Robinson helped Longarm to get down from the buggy. As soon as Longarm was upright, Robinson smoothed and brushed off Longarm's hat and placed it on his head. Then he reached in to help Frank Fools Crow. The Indian needed little help. With controlled dignity, he stepped out of the buggy.

"Listen, Clara," said Longarm to Robinson's wife, still hoping against hope that this pair could not possibly be as insane—or as dangerous—as they sounded. "I told you! I won't press charges!"

"How can we believe that?" she demanded. "Assaulting a federal officer. That *must* be a federal offense."

"Hell, ma'am! What you did was no federal offense! I was on your land, in your barn, taking away your prisoner, and I was holding a gun on you. You did the only sensible thing you could have done, under the circumstances. You deserve a medal, not a criminal citation. Believe me, Mrs. Robinson, there's no need for you to panic like this!"

"You don't understand," said Seth Robinson. "We are not panicking. On the contrary, we are quite used to this sort of thing. You are not the first officer my wife has assaulted. There was a policeman in Denver who tried to carry me off while I was filled with the spirit of the Lord."

"And don't forget, Seth," broke in Clara, "that most abusive constable in St. Louis. Or the one in Cody, two years ago."

Robinson nodded. "Yes, I remember now." The man turned to Longarm and Fools Crow. "Whenever they threaten me with club or gun, Clara—bless her—is moved to a righteous anger. The power of the Great God Jehovah comes upon her."

"My husband," explained Clara, "has found that it is expedient to bring the multitudes to him through his sale of his famous elixir—a health-giving potion designed to cleanse the body, while his words cleanse and refresh their spirits."

"A world-famous tonic," Seth Robinson explained. "Had we met under different circumstances, Deputy, I would have been willing to sell you a bottle. It is made from my own special formula and is guaranteed to purge the ill humors from your body with the goodness of natural spirits and herbs. I have a few cartons left, stored in my barn."

"Excellent for the curing of drug and alcohol addiction," said Clara eagerly, as if she were still speaking from the tailgate of their medicine wagon.

"Clears up piles in no time," added Seth Robinson.

Longarm's head was spinning. He found it difficult to believe in the reality of this addlepated man and woman who were now bent on planting him and Frank Fools Crow on a moonlit hill. He looked at the woman. "What you mean," he said, "is that your husband sold patent medicine as well as the Gospel—but whenever the local law inter-

109

fered, you clobbered them good—the way you just clobbered me."

"You may put it that way if you wish," sniffed Clara Robinson.

"She just stunned you, of course," explained her husband, "but I assure you, when Clara uses something a bit more efficient than a frying pan, she makes a much better job if it."

Clara cleared her throat. She seemed eager to explain to Longarm why this time she had not done her usually efficient job. "Once I used a knife, and another time a poker. But this time I was in too much of a hurry, Deputy. You rode in so quickly after we got back to the farm that I only had time to grab my frying pan."

"I see," said Longarm, glancing nervously at Frank Fools Crow. He saw the light in the Indian's eye and realized that the man was thinking the same thing he was. Together they would have to overpower these two. But how in blazes could they accomplish that with their hands tied securely behind them?

"Hell, Robinson," Longarm said, looking back at the mad couple. "You can let us go right now. You can sell all the snake oil you want, as far as Frank Fools Crow and I are concerned. We won't say a word. In fact, I think that's a grand way of spreading the Gospel among the heathens."

Longarm looked at Frank Fools Crow. "Don't you see it that way too, Fools Crow?"

Fools Crow was ready on the instant. "This Indian feels the spirit of the Great God Jehovah in the air about us," he replied with comical solemnity. "There is no need for violence. Go forth and sell your magic to all who need the light, Seth and Clara Robinson. And let this lawman and Frank Fools Crow go in peace."

Hopefully, Longarm looked back at the pair. But the frowns on their faces told him that their plea had fallen on ears too demented to understand.

Seth's eyes were burning with a fierce, mad light. "The devil speaks through your mouths," he pronounced grimly. As he spoke, he took Longarm's .44 out from under his long frock coat and aimed it at the lawman. "Now, both of you, march ahead of us to the top of this hill."

He turned to his wife. "Get the shovels, Clara," he told her.

She nodded and turned back to the buggy. Nudging Longarm in the back with the barrel of the Colt, Seth started Longarm up the hill, Fools Crow moving just ahead of him.

When they reached the crest, Seth cut their bonds with a hunting knife, then stepped back, holding the .44 trained on them both. Clara arrived, puffing slightly, carrying two spades. She handed one to each of them.

"Dig!" said Robinson.

"For they have done the devil's work!" Clara cried out fiercely, raising her arms to heaven, her pale eyes gleaming now with a fanaticism equal to her husband's.

It was clear to Longarm then that there was no way he could reason with these two. And it was just as plain why they had caught Frank Fools Crow in the first place. Since he was obviously in league with the devil, they had no choice but to visit Jehovah's fury on him, as well. It was the call to Longarm's meeting at the Bar C that had sidetracked them—and eventually netted them another damn fool lawman.

In that instant, Longarm wondered how many other poor unfortunates had fallen into this pair's mad net.

Longarm's spade sliced into the ground. Frank Fools Crow followed Longarm's example, and in a moment the two men were working so steadily that Seth Robinson and his wife began to relax their vigil somewhat. Longarm still had his derringer, but after its failure the day before, when he had pulled it on Murdock, he was reluctant to trust it now, even though he had cleaned it thoroughly since.

Longarm continued to dig, working his way slightly around as he did so until he was within shovel's reach of Seth Robinson. The Indian was no slouch and had been doing the same thing, so that now he was much closer to Robinson as well. Longarm paused, leaned back, and wiped off his forehead. Frank Fools Crow did the same thing.

His purpose in pausing was to catch the Indian's eye and signal him that it was time for them to use their shovels on something other than this rocky soil. One swipe of his spade's blade would catch Robinson neatly on the gun hand, and in a moment the two of them would be on the son of a bitch. Frank Fools Crow caught Longarm's eye and gave a barely perceptible nod. He understood.

But at that moment Seth Robinson moved back a few steps, his wife doing so as well. "Keep those shovels working," Seth warned coldly, "and don't think you can use them to attack either of us. I know what devilish thoughts inhabit your heathen skulls."

Cursing inwardly, Longarm bent once more to his task.

It was only when he glanced wearily to one side a moment later that he saw the glow in the sky. *My God,* he thought, straightening up.

"Look!" he said, pointing to the leaping, pulsing glow. "It's a fire! It looks like it's coming from Cameron's ranch!"

Even as the four of them watched, the glow brightened. At the same moment Longarm heard the dim clatter of hooves coming from the direction of the Robinsons' place. Longarm glanced at their two captors. They had heard the hoofbeats also, and—momentarily confused—were turning from the fire to look back down the hill.

"Now!" cried Longarm, leaping across the trench at Robinson. His head caught the man in the midsection and drove him backward. The man gasped as he tried to keep his feet.

Longarm felt the Indian strike Seth at about the same time, catching him higher—about the shoulders. There was a thunderous roar as the .44 in Robinson's hand detonated. Longarm heard a short, muffled cry from Frank Fools Crow, and the Indian released Robinson. Somehow Robinson managed to stay on his feet; and all the while that Longarm grappled with him in an effort to wrest his Colt from the man's wiry fingers, Clara was pounding him on the back and head with the handle of one of the spades.

At last Longarm managed to bury a punch so deep into Robinson's gut that the man retched and doubled over, clutching at his bowels, the Colt finally dropping from his fingers. But in the darkness Longarm could not find it, and meanwhile, Clara's blows were beginning to take their effect.

Especially when she began using the shovel's blade instead of its handle.

Longarm turned to face her, holding up his left arm to ward off her blows. The blade caught his forearm and dug into it cruelly, driving him down to one knee. He reached into his vest pocket and brought out the derringer.

"I'll fire!" he warned her.

She pulled back, startled. Then her mouth became a firm, angry line. "You wouldn't shoot a defenseless woman!" she cried, and lifted the spade over her head to strike him again.

But Frank Fools Crow had managed by this time to crawl up behind her. With a sudden lunge he grabbed her from behind, bearing her to the ground beneath him. With a startled, furious cry, she tried to wrest herself free. Longarm leaped forward, snatched up the shovel she had dropped, and turned to face Seth Robinson.

Longarm had heard the man rushing toward him. Without pausing as he turned, Longarm swung the blade. It made a high, whistling sound as its edge caught Seth Robinson just under his chin, slicing neatly through his Adam's apple and jugular. The man stopped in his tracks and crumpled to his knees, and with both hands holding on to his severed neck, he sank forward to the ground.

Clara started to scream, but Frank Fools Crow caught her about the mouth, then called in a hoarse whisper to Longarm, "Riders!"

Longarm looked down the hill. In the light of the now-bright moon, he saw four riders milling about the buggy. They did not look to be friendly. Longarm flattened himself on the ground beside Clara and the Indian.

"Who are they?" he asked Fools Crow.

"MacLaggan and his boys, I think."

"That means more trouble. We better get out of here."

Longarm was thinking of that fire lighting the night sky. He was sure it was Harley Cameron's place, and one glance showed that it was still burning furiously. Judging from the fierceness of the glow, it appeared certain that more than one building was afire. And that meant night riders. Simpson Radley and the MacLaggans, it seemed, were now adding their own grim calamities to this wild night.

"I am wounded," Frank Fools Crow said, his voice weak. "Go, Longarm. Save yourself. I will stay here."

"No you won't," Longarm said. "You're coming with me."

At that moment Clara twisted herself free of the Indian's grasp. But before she could call out, Longarm struck her in the jaw with his clenched fist, knocking her senseless. He glanced down the hill. One of the riders had dismounted. It would not be long before they followed the tracks Longarm and the Robinsons had made up to this graveyard.

Retrieving his .44 from the dead Robinson and pulling his hat down tightly, Longarm helped Frank Fools Crow over the crest of the hill and down the other side toward a dark clump of pine. Once they made it to the pines, Longarm held up and looked back. He could see the tombstones outlined clearly against the bright, moonlit sky. A moment later he saw a single figure moving amid the tombstones, and then a horse and rider.

Longarm flung the now unconscious Indian over his back, turned, and began to hurry through the pines. They had just escaped from one trap; he had no intention of getting caught in another.

Chapter 9

Dennis MacLaggan left his horse and walked over to Ed Stoner. The blacksmith turned away from the crumpled figure on the ground, and went over to the weeping Clara Robinson. He knelt on one knee beside her, then helped her gently to her feet. He said to Dennis, "I'll take her down the hill to their buggy."

MacLaggan looked away from Seth Robinson's torn body and nodded absently. "She said that deputy did this, did she?"

"That's right. The Indian too. But she thinks the Indian was hurt."

"What the hell were they doing up here, this hour of the night?"

"I couldn't get that out of her."

MacLaggan nodded, and as Ed led the woman away, he looked back down at the grisly, nearly decapitated corpse of Seth Robinson. He could see at once how it had happened. There had been some digging, and the deputy had swung the spade on Seth.

But what the hell were they doing up here in this graveyard, digging at this hour of the night? Seth Robinson had always struck Dennis as an odd man, and his wife seemed just as strange—but how could there be any logical explanation for this task at such an hour?

Unless, of course, someone was planning on burying someone else!

The moment that thought occurred to him, MacLaggan shook his head incredulously. That could not possibly be what they were up to. But then he looked around once more at the partially dug trenches. Again, he thrust the crazy thought from him and started back to his horse.

He was sure Clara would have an explanation for him as soon as she had pulled herself together. Meanwhile, his boys might as well put those shovels to good use, deepen one of those trenches, and bury the grisly remains of Preacher Robinson.

As MacLaggan stepped into his saddle a moment later, he glanced once more at the glow on the horizon—and swore bitterly. He should have known better than to trust Rad's temper. The crazy fool had obviously set the Cameron ranch ablaze.

Well, Rad sure as hell better not have hurt anyone!

His horse trailing, Dennis sat in the back of the buggy with Clara Robinson, while Ed drove the team. It took awhile before the bereaved woman was able to answer MacLaggan's questions.

"It was that deputy," Clara said. "He was going to bury Seth and me alive," she went on, her voice hushed. "Him and that Indian!"

"But why? What reason had the deputy for doing such a thing?"

"He . . . just hated us." Her head was resting on his shoulder. As she spoke, she looked up at him with wide, fearful eyes still moist from tears.

"Hated you?"

"Yes. He hated us. And the Indian too. They both hated us. They said we were crazy. They drove us up there and told us to start digging."

"What happened then?"

"Seth had a gun. When he pulled it out, the Indian grabbed the shovel away from me and struck Seth with it. Then they ran off."

"Ed said the Indian was hurt."

"Yes." Her eyes glowed suddenly in malignant triumph. "Seth got off a shot. I saw him fall. But then you came, and the two of them ran off."

"The Indian wasn't hurt bad, then."

"The deputy marshal helped him."

Dennis looked down at the mousy Clara Robinson. He had caught something unpleasant and furtive in her eyes, and then, for just a moment, a gleam that startled him with its ferocity.

Or madness.

"Why did he hate you and Seth, Clara?" MacLaggan asked gently. "You can tell me. I'll understand."

She reached up with her left hand and took his shirt front and pulled him close. Then she looked quickly about her. There was no mistaking it this time; her eyes were alight with madness when she glanced back up at him.

"He hated us because we wouldn't give them our secret!"

"Your secret? What was that, Clara?"

"Seth's elixir! The life-giving elixir that only he could make! With it, all ill humors are vanquished from the body and everlasting health is assured! But that deputy marshal was like all the others! He wanted it all for himself!" She was beginning to pant now, and he thought he saw traces of spittle oozing out of one corner of her mouth as her hand gripped his shirt with amazing force.

"And Seth refused the deputy?" MacLaggan prodded.

"Of course! That's why they killed him!"

"You say the deputy marshal was like the others. Which others, Clara?"

"The officer in Denver."

"Any others?"

"The constable in St. Louis. And the sheriff in Cody."

"They were all jealous, were they? They wanted the elixir for themselves, did they?"

She nodded. "That was why they attacked Seth. And why we had to kill them."

"Did you bury them too?"

"Of course."

MacLaggan gently disengaged Clara's hand from his shirt front and leaned back in the leather seat. They were almost to the Robinson's farm. He wondered how much of this conversation Ed Stoner had heard above the rattle of the buggy.

Then they were wheeling in off the road, through the gate, and into the farm's front yard. Ed reined up in front of the barn.

As he did so, Seth's boy Jed and one of his hired hands emerged from the barn. It was obvious that after sending Dennis and his men after the Robinsons earlier, they had been waiting anxiously for their return.

The moment Clara saw her son, she flung herself from the buggy and into his arms. It took a few minutes for Dennis to explain to the boy what he knew, since Clara's renewed grief made her almost totally incoherent. Then Dennis told Jed to take his mother into the house and do his best to settle her down some.

As the boy left for the house with his wailing mother, Dennis called the hired man over to him. Dennis did not care much for his looks. The fellow's face was round and seemed to have the consistency of bread dough. Grossly overweight, he favored bright yellow suspenders.

"When we rode in here earlier," MacLaggan began, "Jed told us his folks had been kidnapped by the deputy and the Indian."

The man nodded.

"Just let me get this straight," Dennis said carefully, studying the hired man very closely. "The deputy and the Indian *kidnapped* Seth and Clara?"

Again the round fellow nodded. But perhaps not as emphatically as before.

"In a *buggy?*"

His dull eyes growing furtive, the fellow cleared his throat. "Yes," he said, his voice barely audible.

He reminded Dennis of an animal that had just emerged from darkness into daylight and was about ready to dart back into his den again.

"Doesn't that seem strange to you?"

"No, sir," the hired man said, his eyes glancing quickly from Dennis to Ed Stoner and back again. "It don't."

Dennis considered this sorry human specimen for a moment longer. He wasn't even a good liar. MacLaggan decided to take another tack.

"Clara wants to thank me," Dennis told the man. "She said I could have a few bottles of the preacher's elixir for my men. Can you take me to them?"

The man hesitated for only an instant, then nodded, turned, and headed into the barn. Dennis turned to Ed Stoner and invited him along.

They followed the hired man through the barn to a storeroom in the back. The fellow pulled the door open and led the way into the room. Lifting a lantern off a nail on the wall, he lit it, adjusted the wick, then hung the lantern back up.

In the dim yellow light, Dennis saw before him case upon case of the elixir, piled almost to the rafters. And on the floor in one corner lay a second hired man. This worthy was flat on his back, snoring softly, an empty bottle of "elixir" in his hand. Everywhere Dennis looked, he saw empty bottles of the preacher's cure-all littering the straw-covered floor.

Picking up a bottle of what the label called Professor Robinson's World-Famous Elixir, Dennis put the neck of the empty bottle to his nose. The smell was not unpleasant— and his senses reeled slightly as he inhaled. The concoction that had filled this bottle appeared to have been compounded of laudanum, alcohol, sugar, and perhaps a little ginger.

The odor was a familiar one to him, he realized at once. He had smelled it on Clara when she had leaned her head on his shoulder, on the hired hand as he led them through the barn, and quite possibly on Clara's son, as well. The whole damned pack of them were more or less permanently soused on this evil concoction of the preacher's. No wonder that self-righteous son of a bitch was so all-fired anxious to point the finger of damnation at MacLaggan and the rest of them. Hellfire, their whiskey was possibly the only real competition his damned elixir had in this high country.

He shook his head, and found himself wondering if he would ever find out how many of Preacher Robinson's congregation were taking his elixir—instead of MacLaggan's whiskey.

"There sure as hell is enough of the stuff," said Ed Stoner.

"Yes. There is at that."

"You believe that cock-and-bull story that woman told you in the buggy, Dennis?"

"What do you think?"

"I think she's as mad as a hatter."

"Yes. I am afraid so. And her late husband as well."

"Let's get out of here."

MacLaggan nodded and left the storeroom. A moment later, just as they emerged from the barn, Rad and his men galloped through the farm's gate and pulled to a sliding halt before him. Rad flung himself from his lathered mount.

"Where is he?" he demanded. "Where's that damned Indian?"

"He's gone. With that deputy marshal."

"What the hell happened?"

"That's a long story. What I want to know, Rad, is what happened at the Bar C."

"Cameron tried to save that slut and came at Dudley with a weapon," he lied boldly, knowing neither Dudley nor anyone else sitting their horses behind him would dare contradict his account. "So he shot the son of a bitch."

"Is he dead?"

"He's dead."

MacLaggan groaned inwardly. "And then you burned his house and barns for good measure."

"That wasn't my fault. His hired hands opened up on us. Hell, Dennis, we was lucky to get out of that place alive."

"I think we've done enough damage for one night, Rad. I'm for heading back to my place as soon as my boys get back here."

"Just tell me which way that Indian went."

Wearily, MacLaggan waved in the general direction of the hilltop graveyard they had just left.

"Hellfire, Dennis! That ain't no help!"

"I didn't think it would be."

"You goin' to tell me what happened?"

"Inside," MacLaggan said. "I need something in my stomach. I'll tell you while I wait for my boys."

Reluctantly, Rad headed for the farmhouse with MacLaggan.

Behind them, his weary riders dismounted to wait. Dudley Withers swore softly, stretched slowly, then leaned back against the barn and rolled himself a cigarette.

This sure had been one hell of a night, he told himself. Then he thought of that girl he had pistol-whipped and the man he had shot—and took a long drag on his cigarette, wondering why the thought gave him no pleasure—why, instead, he felt only a bone-deep chill that, despite the cigarette, seemed to be spreading through his vitals.

It was midmorning when Longarm reached a stream and lowered Frank Fools Crow to the ground as gently as he could. He had traveled through the night and most of that morning with the Indian draped over his shoulders. After both men had drunk their fill of the ice-cold stream, Longarm leaned wearily back against a sapling and took out a cheroot. Lighting it, he offered it to Frank Fools Crow and told the Indian to smoke it while he examined the Indian's wound a second time.

The hole the .44 slug had made in the Indian's shoulder was a big one, and there was no sign of an exit wound. The slug was still in there somewhere. Longarm had been able to stanch the blood flow by ripping his shirt into strips and binding the wound as tightly as the Indian could stand it. This was difficult to tell, however, since Frank Fools Crow refused to cry out, no matter what the provocation.

Longarm unwound the bandage and inspected the entry wound. It looked inflamed already. And as he probed the area around it, a thin trickle of greenish fluid oozed out of the blackening hole.

"We got to get that bullet out and clean up that wound," Longarm said.

"Yes," said Fools Crow.

"We should be close to Cameron's spread. If they were able to save anything from that fire, I'm hoping it was horseflesh and a wagon."

"Where will you go with a wagon?"

"To Red Gap. There must be a doctor there who can get that bullet out."

"A white doctor?"

"Yes."

"There is one. He lives on whiskey. His hand trembles. He will finish what that crazy Robinson started. It is a shame. You work so hard to save me. You are a good friend."

"Hell, you saved me, don't forget."

"That is right. But you were not doomed. I caused Silver Hump's death. It will do you no good to carry me any farther. I am a dead man already."

"I don't believe that. I believe in other medicine, the white man's medicine."

Fools Crow nodded solemnly. "I understand. I have white blood in me also. This is maybe why I let you help me. I do not know myself. The white blood fights the red blood." He sighed. "We will see who wins."

Longarm finished rewrapping Fools Crow's wound, took a deep breath, and got to his feet.

"We've got to get going."

The cheroot still in his mouth, Fools Crow allowed himself to be slung over Longarm's back. A moment later they were on their way, following the stream downhill.

It was less than an hour later when Longarm topped a low ridge and found himself with a clear view of what was left of the Bar C. Both barns and the ranch house were gutted, the blackened ruins still smoldering. Just the fireplace and chimney were left of the ranch house. The only structure that had survived without damage was the small bunkhouse.

Longarm swore angrily, expecting some kind of a response from Fools Crow. But there was none. He jostled the man slightly to see if he was still conscious. There was a barely perceptible response from the wounded man. Close to exhaustion by this time, Longarm started up again, picking his way carefully down the long slope toward the flat below.

He was halfway across the Bar C compound when Pete Geller, Cameron's hand, emerged from the bunkhouse and hurried toward him. Behind him came Faith Cameron. She called out a faint, listless greeting to Longarm, and stayed in the doorway. One look at her drawn face told Longarm that the Camerons had lost more than a few buildings.

As soon as Pete reached Longarm, he took the Indian off Longarm's back. Frank Fools Crow came awake then, but just barely. They each took an arm and helped the Indian walk unsteadily toward the bunkhouse.

"What happened, Pete? How'd the fire get started?"

"It was set, Mr. Long. By Radley and his men. They was lookin' for you and this Indian."

"Where's Harley? Was he hurt in the fire?"

"Harley's dead, but it wasn't the fire killed him."

"What happened?"

"Dudley Withers. He shot him."

Longarm swore softly, shaking his head.

"And that ain't all."

"You mean the children were hurt?"

"No. The children are all right. It's Annabelle Svenson. She was shot by one of Rad's men as they rode out."

"How badly was she hurt?"

"She's dead too, Mr. Long. The bullet went clean through her head."

They were at the bunkhouse by this time. Faith Cameron stepped out of the doorway and helped them lead the groggy Indian inside and over to a bunk. The four Cameron children were huddled in a corner of the bunkhouse, talking softly among themselves. They looked dispiritedly over at Longarm as he helped Faith undo Fools Crow's bandage. While she worked, Pete held out a jug of moonshine to the Indian.

Frank Fools Crow pushed it away.

"Indian and firewater don't mix," he said softly. Then he looked at Longarm. "My spirit asks for one more of your smokes, Longarm."

Longarm lit a fresh cheroot for the Indian and placed it between his lips.

"All right, then," said Longarm. "This is for your spirit. Not for you."

"My spirit thanks you," said the Indian, a twinkle in his dark eyes despite the pain Longarm saw there as well.

Puffing contentedly, Frank Fools Crow closed his eyes—and a moment later passed out. Longarm took the cheroot from his mouth, stubbed it out carefully, and left it on a crate beside the bunk.

"For when he wakes up," he told Faith.

She just nodded, so intent was she on cleaning out the Indian's wound. She was using a harsh-smelling bar of yellow soap and a saucepan of hot water she had obtained in an astonishingly short time. He could see that working with this intensity over Frank Fools Crow was helping her fight the enormous grief she still felt for the death of her husband.

He left her and walked over to Pete Geller. He suggested they leave the bunkhouse. Pete nodded. Outside, they leaned back against the bunkhouse, and Longarm took out two cheroots and handed one to Pete. After they had lit up, Longarm asked, "What were you able to save from the barn?"

"The horses, most of the saddles, and a couple of wagons. Mr. Cameron's sulky we were not able to save, though. It was in too far back."

"He won't be missing it."

"No."

"Tell me about it."

Pete took a deep breath and related what he had seen from outside. When he heard the shot from within the ranch house, he and the other two hands had armed themselves and started for it. Before they reached it, however, the flames erupted, the door opened, and Radley and his men boiled out. As soon as Rad's men began shooting, Bo and Will broke off and ran into the darkness for cover. Pete had no choice but to follow while Withers and Rad set fire to the barns. By that time Pete was firing back at them from behind the bunkhouse. Yelling like crazy men, Rad and his men rode off, shooting wildly at random targets.

It was that last flurry of gunfire that caught Annabelle.

"Clear through the head, you said."

Pete nodded solemnly.

"And it was Dudley Withers who shot Cameron."

"That's what I got out of the missus. Harley had pulled Withers off Annabelle. Guess Withers was beating up on her real bad. Harley came over and tried to stop him. He started punching him and Withers just pulled out his gun and shot him. Harley was gutshot, Marshal. He was lucky he died so quick. We buried them both this morning."

"Where?"

Pete turned and pointed to a slight rise beyond one of the burned-out barns. Longarm saw two makeshift crosses side by side, a fresh mound of dark earth before each one.

Annabelle and Harley Cameron, lying together in death. It was, Longarm thought, an ironic conclusion to their illicit affair.

He looked back at Pete. "I'll want two wagons for Faith and her children and for the Indian. You and I will need two mounts. Get the wagons ready and saddle up the horses. We're heading for Red Gap before this hour is up."

Pete appeared pleased to have someone give him a direct order once again. With a quick nod he started for the rope corral behind the bunkhouse, where the horses and wagons had been left.

Longarm went back into the bunkhouse to tell Faith his plans.

It was close to sundown when Longarm entered Red Gap and put Cameron's widow and her four children up at the hotel, at his expense. Then, while Will drove, he and Pete Geller accompanied the wagon containing the now-unconscious Frank Fools Crow to the barbershop, above which Red Gap's lone doctor was said to have his office.

Bo had been sent by Longarm to the Box H and the Lazy S to acquaint them with what Radley and his men had done to the Bar C, and to alert them to Radley's presence in their area. He had also instructed Bo to tell them he was taking Faith and her children to Red Gap, and that he expected trouble once Radley discovered his—and the Indian's—whereabouts. He was leaving what action they should take up to them.

Longarm was under no illusions as to what help he could expect from the ranchers, but that didn't matter. At least he had warned them.

A small crowd of curious townsfolk gathered as soon as they pulled up in front of the barbershop, and many soon pressed close enough to peer into the wagon at the long body of the Indian stretched out on the straw mattress. The news that Frank Fools Crow had been brought into town, wounded, raced swiftly through the crowd. As Longarm left the wagon and started up the outside flight of steps to the doctor's office, he saw a gangling youngster racing from the crowd. To spread the news, Longarm had no doubt.

He paused on the landing to read the neat, hand-painted sign nailed to the door: DOCTOR LYLE RAMSDELL. Longarm knocked once, then pushed open the door. He found himself confronting a tall, spare man with gaunt, prominent cheekbones, and eyes that seemed to be looking out at the world from the depths of an ancient despair. He held his doctor's bag in his right hand and was in the act of putting his hat on when Longarm entered. For a moment the doctor swayed unsteadily. The strong odor of stale whiskey filled the musty, cluttered office. Longarm was not impressed.

"I'm Deputy U.S. Marshal Custis Long, Doc," Longarm said. "I've got a patient for you."

"Yes, Marshal. I am aware of that. I was on my way down to see the patient," the doctor replied. "How badly is he hurt?"

"It's a gunshot wound. The slug is still in him."

"Is he feverish?"

"Yes."

"Then perhaps it would be better if you could bring him up here at once. I have a cot in the back room."

Longarm turned, stepped out on the landing, and told Pete and Will to bring Fools Crow up. In a moment, carrying the Indian between them, the two men appeared in the office doorway. The doctor led them quickly past his desk and into the small back room. He had already placed a fresh blanket on the cot. Carefully the two men laid the unconscious man down, then stepped back.

Watching from the doorway, Longarm saw the doctor's long fingers swiftly undo the bandage. As soon as the man had inspected the wound, he glanced up at Longarm. "I will have to go in after the bullet."

"I figured that, Doc."

"I'll need help. Can you hold him down?"

"We can," Longarm said, indicating Pete and Will with a nod.

"Good. But first I must wash my hands."

Longarm watched the man pour a strong-smelling liquid into a large washbowl, mix it with warm water he had simmering on a woodstove in back, then wash his hands up to his elbows in the mixture. Pete made a face and looked away. The acrid, acidic smell obviously bothered him.

"What is that stuff, Doc?" Longarm asked, curious.

"Carbolic acid and water." The man glanced up as he toweled himself off with a surprisingly clean towel. "Have you heard of Joseph Lister?"

"Nope."

"Nor Semmelweis, either, I presume."

"That's right, Doc."

"Well, I have. The idea, Marshal, is to prevent further infection as I probe for the bullet. I see the wound has already been cleansed. Did you do that?"

"Nope. Faith Cameron."

"She did an excellent job."

"All she used was soap and water, Doc."

"For her purposes, that was an excellent choice."

The doctor took a scalpel and a few other surgical instruments out of his bag, dipped them into the bowl of carbolic acid solution, then carefully placed them in a shiny metal tray resting on a small table beside the cot. Apparently ready now to proceed, he beckoned to Longarm to hold Fools Crow down. Longarm and the two others stationed themselves alongside the bed. With a nod, Longarm indicated that Pete and Will should hold the Indian's legs while

127

he held him by the shoulders.

When they were ready, Longarm glanced at the doctor. "Now, Doc."

The man sliced deftly, laying back the flesh, then probed deeply. He grunted after a moment when he felt something, then he reached back to the tray for a long, tweezerlike instrument, probed carefully for a moment longer, and withdrew the almost flattened slug and dropped it into the tray.

Swiftly the doctor swabbed the wound out with the carbolic acid solution, then began to sew the Indian up. He had a difficult time; his fingers had begun to shake, and Fools Crow was bleeding heavily. But at least, Longarm noted, the blood was red and clean; no longer was that greenish fluid issuing from the wound. Once the stitches were in place, the doctor placed a bandage saturated with the solution over the wound, and then, using fresh bandages, bound it securely, stanching the flow of blood.

Longarm and the others stepped away from the cot. Fools Crow opened his eyes and looked over at the doctor. "You did not need to hold down Fools Crow," he said. "From the beginning, I know your white medicine is great magic. Maybe the whiskey help. Someday, perhaps, my medicine will be as great as yours, Doctor."

"You mean you were conscious all during the operation?" the doctor asked incredulously.

"Yes. I want to know how you reach into my body and take from it the burning piece of lead. It was very deep, Doctor."

"Yes, it was in there, all right. But fortunately it had missed your lung. An inch or two to the right, and you would not have been so lucky."

Fools Crow looked over at Longarm. "Now maybe I have one of those fine smokes."

Laughing, Longarm passed him a cheroot and lit it for him. The doctor cleared away his instruments and the carbolic acid solution, then went quickly into his office. Pulling open a desk drawer, he hauled a jug of moonshine up onto the desk. Longarm followed.

"Pour me some too, Doc," he said. "That was a nice job. I have a hunch that crazy Indian is going to live."

Smiling for the first time, the doctor filled a tall mug for Longarm and one for himself. "Let's hope so," the man said, raising the mug to Longarm in salute.

Longarm drank up. It was like downing a kerosene fire. But he blinked once or twice, then put the mug back down on the desk for more. The doctor had saved Frank Fools Crow's life, it appeared, but Longarm was aware that the battle to keep Frank Fools Crow alive in this country was not over yet, not by a damn sight.

But if the Radleys and MacLaggans had a score to settle with Frank Fools Crow, Longarm had one to settle with them, as well.

Chapter 10

Cal Hardman watched with his three sons as Bo rode out on his way to the Lazy S. He was standing in the doorway to his ranch house. Behind him, he heard his wife, Jennifer, approach the door, and he turned to face her.

"We'll just sit tight, Jen," he told her. "Don't you worry none. There ain't no reason for us to risk tangling with the Radleys and MacLaggans to save an Indian and that fool deputy marshal."

Cal's three sons nodded solemnly.

"But wasn't that awful," Jennifer said, "about poor Harley? What a terrible thing."

"That's what happens when you meddle, Ma," said the oldest Hardman boy. His name was Wesley. He had a narrow face, a wide mouth, and eyes set pretty far apart. It reminded most people of a horse's face when they first saw him, and his mother, as a result, felt more maternal and protective toward him than she did toward her other two sons. She knew how difficult it would be for him to live down his horseface. Her uncle Horace had had such a face, and he never did get married.

"You're right, Wesley," she said. "But still, you must wonder if this terrible man, Radley, can be controlled."

"There's no reason for him to bother us," said Anthony. He was taller and a year older than Wesley, and his features were comely and pleasant to look upon, his voice a delight, like Jennifer's mother's. "We don't know where that Indian is, and we don't care."

"I suppose," said Jennifer uncertainly. She looked at her third boy, Wallace. "What do you think, Wally?"

Wallace, twenty-one, was the youngest, and he never liked to agree immediately with his brothers—not until he knew which way his parents were leaning. He looked nervously at his father. "I agree with Dad. They ain't no reason to get mixed up in this. Who cares about an Indian and a deputy marshal anyway? Ain't that right, Dad?"

"That's the way I feel about it," Cal replied, nodding his head emphatically. "And I don't think Bo's going to have any luck draggin' Matt into this, either. Now let's all get inside and finish that meal your mother done fixed us."

The four of them hurried back inside, sat themselves back down at the table, and set to work on their noon meal with a cheerful gusto that, as usual, made Jennifer Hardman proud.

About half an hour later, as Jennifer finished washing the dishes, she heard the sudden clatter of hoofbeats. She looked over at her husband, who was busy polishing his shotgun. Cal put the rag on the table and went to the door, still carrying the shotgun.

Pulling it open, he stepped out into the bright afternoon sunlight. Jennifer followed out after him. The three boys were just emerging from the barn. The front yard was thick with dust from the riders who had just pulled up. As the dust settled, Cal saw Rad and his two sons and Dudley Withers.

"Howdy, Rad," Cal said. "Light and rest a spell. All of you. Jen'll put some coffee on. Won't take a minute."

Rad heaved himself off his horse and walked toward Cal. He did not look at all friendly. "That ain't no way to invite a man into your house. Fact is, that's downright unfriendly."

"Why . . . what do you mean, Rad?"

By that time Rad had reached Cal. With a quick movement he snatched the shotgun out of Cal's hands, turned, and tossed it up to Dudley Withers, who had let his horse follow behind Rad as he approached Cal. Dudley snatched the shotgun out of the air and set it across his pommel, a grin on his mean face.

Cal didn't like that at all. "Now see here, Rad! You got no call to ride in here and—"

Rad cut his words short with a vicious slap that almost sent Cal to the ground. His eyes stinging with tears, rage pushed aside whatever good sense Cal had left, and he lunged for Rad. Rad stepped lightly out of his way and brought the barrel of his sixgun down on the top of Cal's head.

The next thing Cal knew, he was looking dazedly up at Rad, the top of his head throbbing. Warm, sticky blood was oozing down the right side of his face. His mouth dry, he tried to speak. But he could not articulate. Rad, looking down at him, laughed.

Rad's two boys and Dudley had dismounted by that time, and while Cal watched helplessly, his three boys, guns held on them by Rad's sons, were herded roughly past him into the house. When Jennifer protested, Dudley simply shoved the barrel of his sixgun brutally into her back. Cal heard her startled cry as she stumbled momentarily, then half ran into the ranch house behind her boys.

"We're hungry, Hardman," Radley said, holstering his weapon. "Hear tell that woman of yours sets a fine table. Get up now and go on in there. You look like you could use that coffee you mentioned."

Cal pushed himself upright. His knees threatened to collapse under him as he started for the ranch house, but he managed to stay on his feet. Reaching one hand out to take the doorjamb, he eased himself through the doorway and saw Dudley and Rad's two boys sitting at his kitchen table. His own three sons were huddled in the corner, watching, while Jennifer, her hands visibly trembling, spooned grounds into the coffeepot and saw to the fire in the stove.

Behind him, Rad shoved him viciously. Stumbling headlong into the house, Cal only just caught himself by grabbing hold of a chair. Rad strode in past him and sat down at the kitchen table.

"Get over here, Hardman," he said. "I want to talk to you."

Cal moistened his dry lips. He wanted nothing more than to kill the four men sitting at his table. But he knew that he was no match for them, that they would kill him without the flicker of an eye if he gave them any trouble, real or imagined. The taste of fear was in his mouth and he swallowed miserably as he shuffled over to the table and came to a halt beside Radley. What hurt the most was that his three sons were witnessing his disgrace.

"We saw you coming from the Bar C—the whole damn pack of you," Rad snarled. "There's no use in denying it. That Svenson whore was in there, and so was that deputy marshal. You was all cookin' up a scheme to stop me and MacLaggan, weren't you?"

Cal cleared his throat, anxious to set matters straight. "Now listen, Rad, that ain't—"

"You shut up and you listen, Hardman! Don't you try to weasel out of it none. I saw you and MacLaggan saw you."

"All right. So you saw us! What do you want now?"

"You know goddamn well what I want! I want to know where that half-breed and that deputy marshal are. And you better tell me. MacLaggan said they were headed this way."

Cal felt an enormous flood of relief. "I'll tell you," he said. "I'll tell you where they are. But I'll be damned if I'll do it under your gun! You got no right to come in here like this and shove me and my wife around!"

Rad took out his gun, cocked it, aimed it at a spot between Cal's eyes, shifted the barrel up a few inches—and pulled the trigger. The detonation filled the room with a thunderous roar, and Cal felt the bullet plowing through the air just above his head. It burrowed harmlessly into a rafter above his head. Rad had never intended to kill him, but the effect on Cal was astounding. He felt himself trembling, his knees gave out, and he had to reach over to the table to keep himself on his feet.

"Now you listen here to me, Hardman. Don't you go

givin' *me* orders. You just tell me where I can find them two—and be quick about it, or we'll let my boys here practice on your boys for a while." He grinned then. "And maybe let Dudley have a taste of Jennifer here."

Cal's head spun. He was feeling both a numbing, paralyzing fear and a rage that astonished him with its vehemence. He wanted to reach out and strangle Rad so badly that it made him weak. But at the same time he wanted Rad, his boys, and Dudley to ride off his place and leave him in peace.

Rad stood up suddenly and pushed Cal away from the table. Again, he cocked his sixgun. This time he thrust it into Cal's midsection and grinned. "All right, Hardman. Tell me. Where are they?"

"In Red Gap," Cal told him, his voice thick with rage.

"How the hell could that be?" Rad thrust the barrel still deeper into Cal's gut. "What are you tryin' to tell me? I warn you, Hardman. You send me on any wild-goose chase, I'll come back here and roast you alive and eat your guts out in front of your wife and children!"

It was a preposterous threat, but the maniacal light in Rad's eye convinced Cal completely. He almost peed in his pants in his eagerness to convince Rad that what he was telling him was the truth.

"It's the truth, I tell you!" he cried. "The Indian was wounded bad, and the deputy took him and Cameron's widow into Red Gap. Bo rode in from Red Gap just before you did! Isn't that right, Jennifer?"

The woman nodded, her eyes wide. She had long since given up trying to heat fresh coffee for the intruders. She was too terrified.

"Bo?" Rad's eyes narrowed. "You mean Cameron's hired man?"

"Yes. It was Bo rode in here. That marshal sent him to warn me and Matt Stokes that you might be in the area, looking for him and the Indian. He wanted to warn us . . . and to ask us to throw in with him."

Aware that he was almost babbling in his frantic eagerness to spill what he knew to this bullying brute before him, Cal held up for a second and glanced unhappily over at his three sons. They looked away from him, unwilling to let their eyes meet his. They were ashamed of him. They *pitied* him!"

'Rad shoved the barrel of his sixgun still deeper into Cal's gut. "I believe you. It makes sense, now that I think of it. You're in cahoots with them bastards, so he was calling for help. And I'll bet you was getting ready to saddle up and ride to Red Gap when I rode in, wasn't you?"

"No!" cried Cal. "I wasn't! This ain't none of my fight. I told Bo that. Honest, Rad. Honest to God!"

Rad looked at him for a long moment, then gathered saliva in his mouth and spat full in Cal's face. "You're a liar!" he exploded. "A goddamn liar! If it wasn't that I pity your poor sniveling cubs in the corner, I'd kill you right here and now! Just like that Indian killed my own two sons!"

"Oh Jesus, Cal! I had nothing to do with the death of your two boys! I didn't know nothin' about that! You got to believe me!"

"I don't *got* to do nothin'," Rad replied, holstering his weapon suddenly and sitting back down in his chair. "Now where the hell's that coffee? And that meal?"

As he spoke, he turned about and glared at Jennifer.

The poor woman almost cried out in terror. But she caught herself and began to shove kindling frantically into the stove's belly. She was close to collapsing, so frightened was she. As he watched her, Cal felt the spittle running down his face, dripping off his chin. His boys had turned away in shame. At that moment something burst within Cal, and all restraint—all good sense—vanished.

"Damn you!" Cal cried, throwing himself with sudden fury on Radley. "Damn you all to hell!"

The force of his lunge swept Radley and his chair over onto its back. Cal came down hard on Radley. He saw the look of pure surprise on the man's face, and gained heart as his fingers began to close about the man's neck. He saw Rad gasping for breath, his eyes bugging out. But even as his fingers tightened their grip, he knew he had committed a terrible error, that he had doomed himself.

The shadow of Dudley Withers fell over them. Cal started to glance back, but he was not in time to prevent the barrel of Dudley's revolver from smashing down—hard—on the same spot on the top of the skull where Rad had hit him before. As Cal's fingers relaxed from around Rad's neck, he felt himself slipping away, then falling into a bottomless pit from which he knew instinctively there would be no return.

And he was right. Before he rolled off Radley, he was a dead man.

Bo Allen rode tall in his saddle, tall and easy, as befit a man who had spent a lifetime astride one horse or another. The moment he broke out of the pines, he spotted below him the scattering of low buildings that made up the Lazy S. But he did not urge his horse to go any faster as it angled down the long slope. He didn't see any need for haste.

Bo was in his late forties, though he wasn't absolutely sure just how late that was. He was a wiry fellow with a prominent Adam's apple, light hazel eyes, and a considerable mop of graying hair that poked out from under his black Stetson. There was little to distinguish him from any other cowhand that drifted from ranch to ranch. Like the rest of his kind, Bo always managed to find a reason for moving on, but never really knew why he did.

He had planned on giving his notice to Harley Cameron next spring, but it looked now as if he'd be moving on a mite sooner. Bo had liked Cameron and those four kids of his, especially. But he had long since determined he would never let himself get too close to the men he worked for, so he felt only a sadness—together with an infinite weariness—that always came over him when he knew he had to ride out and find another chuckwagon to follow.

That was why he didn't mind this job of warning the other ranchers. It gave him something to do, and it was something that might help matters. He didn't mind not having been much help to Cameron during his trouble, since he didn't see what he could have done under the circumstances. But this much, at least, he could do.

Not that he expected Cal Hardman to do anything to help that deputy marshal. And he didn't think Matthew Stokes would be any more willing to help the lawman, either. Of course, there was always Matt's grandfather. Now *there* was someone, Bo thought with a chuckle, who might be more than willing to throw in with Deputy Long. If he could get over his bone-deep hatred of redskins, that is.

When he rode into the Lazy S compound, Matt Stokes and his foreman, Bull Sweet, were walking across the compound to greet him. Bo pulled up and folded his arms wearily across the pommel of his saddle.

"Howdy, Matt, Bull," he said.

"Light and set a spell, Bo," said Matt.

Bo dismounted wearily, took off his hat and used it to beat the dust from his Levi's, then led his horse to the hitch rail in front of the ranch house, as Matt and Bull accompanied him.

"What brings you out here, Bo?" Matt asked. It was obvious to Bo that Matt sensed trouble.

Carefully, Bo draped the reins of his horse over the hitch rail and started up the short flight of steps leading to the veranda. "Harley Cameron's dead, Matt."

"What's that you say, Bo?" Matt asked, incredulous. "Harley? Dead?"

"You heard me right," Bo said, folding his long frame into a wicker rocking chair on the veranda and taking out a plug of tobacco. "One of Rad's men killed him," he went on, biting off a fair-sized chunk. "Dudley Withers. They also killed the Svenson woman. Right now Rad's on the warpath, and he might be here pretty soon. That Marshal Long sent me to warn you—and also to see if maybe now you might be willing to throw in with him—now that you seen what you're up against."

"I can't believe it," Matt said. He had stopped in the act of mounting the steps. He stood now on the top step, staring at Bo.

"You can believe it, all right," Bo said, chewing carefully. "I was there. I saw the whole thing."

"Tell me about it."

So Bo told him.

When he was done, Matt finished mounting the steps and went inside the house. Bull Sweet, leaning against the hitch rail, had listened intently as well. He cleared his throat.

"You told Cal Hardman about this?" he asked.

"I told him."

"He throwin' in with the deputy marshal and that Indian?"

"I wouldn't bet on it." Bo sent a dark stream of tobacco juice off the veranda. It struck the dust of the yard with a soft splat.

"He's an old woman," Bull said.

Bo said nothing to contradict that as he leaned back in the rocker. After a moment, Matt's grandfather appeared with a cup of hot coffee and a wedge of apple pie that Bo knew the old man had made himself. He put them down on a small table by the rocker and went back inside.

The coffee was just right, thick enough to stand a spoon up straight, and the pie was better than delicious. The Lazy S had no women. Matt's wife had died nearly fifteen years before, and had left him no children to remember her by. There was no trace of a woman's hand anywhere about the place. No curtains on the windows. No rugs on the floor. No flowers bordering the house. But that didn't mean that Matt and Gramps didn't see to it that the ranch house was kept spotless. Indeed, it fairly shone. Bo always liked coming here. It was a comfortable place for a man. Peaceable.

Matt returned to the veranda. His sixgun was strapped to his hip and he was carrying his Winchester. A blanket roll was slung over his shoulder.

"I'll be ridin' back to Red Gap with you," he said to Bo. Then he looked down at his foreman. "I want you to stay here with Gramps, Bull. There ain't no reason for you to come along on this. In fact, I'd take it as downright unfriendly if you didn't want to stay here and look after Gramps."

"I'll stay, Matt," Bull said, smiling. "You don't have to pull a gun on me. I don't mind lookin' after the old man."

"I just don't want him alone with Vinegar Bill and Jack if that murderin' son of a bitch shows up here."

"I'll keep an eye out, Matt. Don't worry."

"That's settled, then," Matt said, turning to Bo. "You ready?"

"As ready as I'll ever be," Bo replied, reluctantly getting up from the rocker.

Bo was mounted up and Matt was leading his black out of the barn, already saddled, when they both heard, the mutter of horses' hooves. They turned toward the sound and saw Rad and three other riders streaming down the slope, heading for the Lazy S.

Matt shouted into the barn for Bull to get Gramps hid. Bull darted from the barn to the ranch house. A moment later, Bo heard the back door slam shut. Matt was sure taking Gramps out of harm's way. At the same time, Matt's two hired hands appeared in the barn doorway.

"Arm yourselves," Matt told them.

They raced across the compound to the bunkhouse.

Rad and his three riders galloped into the compound, slowing down only when they saw Matt level his Winchester on Rad and track him as he rode closer. Matt was standing behind his black, resting the Winchester on the animal's rump.

"Now what's this?" Rad asked, reining in. "A fine way to greet a neighbor, I'm thinking."

"You ain't a neighbor, Rad. You're a mad dog runnin' loose. A killer. Turn that horse around and ride out of here, or I'll blow you off it."

"I do believe you mean it."

"You're damn right I mean it."

Rad looked at Bo. "What you been tellin' Matt, Bo?"

"The truth."

"And what might that be?"

"That you killed Harley Cameron and the Svenson girl."

"It wasn't me killed Harley, Matt," said Rad. "It was Dudley here. He had no choice. Harley pulled a gun on him. And that Svenson woman was just a piece of trash— a high-priced whore who gave herself airs."

"Where's your partner, Rad?" Matt asked. "Where's MacLaggan? Did he run out on you?"

"He didn't have the stomach for what has to be done. But I don't need him, Matt, and if I was you, I'd put down that rifle. I might get riled."

"I got no reason to trust you, Rad. Not after what I just heard."

Rad's face suddenly darkened. "Damn you! You don't

140

understand! I lost two sons to that damned Indian and his marshal friend. Lester and Lafe! Both of them! And Miles Farnum, Scofield, and Dill Williams! I been wiped out by them two—and I mean to see justice done!"

"So you killed Harley Cameron and that girl."

"It don't matter who I kill, so long as I get those two. And it don't matter how many, neither."

Something in the way Rad said this made Bo shudder. Simpson Radley was no longer a very sane man, Bo realized. He let his hand fall to his sidearm.

Radley saw the movement of Bo's hand and smiled coldly. "I know where they are, Bo," he said. "In Red Gap. But I'm here to see that you and Matt don't join him. I've already seen to Cal Hardman."

"What the hell have you done to Cal?" Matt asked.

"Never mind that. Just put down that rifle, Matt—unless of course you're willin' to use it."

Matt moistened his suddenly dry lips. "Why, damn you. You know I'll use this if I have to."

"I don't know nothing of the sort," said Rad, leaning suddenly closer.

Matt tried to lower the barrel of his rifle to keep his sights on Rad, but as he did so, Rad flung himself from his mount, his sixgun materializing in his right hand. It was spitting fire even before Rad struck the ground. He was firing into Matt's black, and brought it down almost at once with two rounds into its massive chest.

As the horse crumpled, Rad shot Matt in the head. Bo saw Matt's hat fly off as he went for his own gun. But he had never drawn a gun in anger in his life. He was still clawing for his weapon when Rad's first bullet struck him in the chest and sent him flying back off his horse.

He hit the ground hard and lay spread-eagled on his back, his breath knocked out of him, unable to move. Dudley's figure loomed between him and the dazzling blue sky. The sixgun in his hand gleamed. Bo tried to raise his right hand to ward off what he knew was coming, but all the lines were down. Dudley fired twice. Each round was an enormous fist pounding him into the ground.

Bo knew he was a dead man. As he drifted off, he was

surprised that he felt no pain—only a strange relief. This was the last time he would be moving on. His rootless days of wandering were over at last. . . .

Radley was walking over to inspect the wounded Stokes when gunfire erupted from the bunkhouse. At once Abe cried out and tumbled from his horse. Abe's older brother Link scrambled from his mount, the rifle at his shoulder blazing as Dudley flung himself from his mount and, using the dead horse for cover, began pouring a steady, murderous fusillade into the bunkhouse.

The moment Radley heard his youngest boy's cry, he turned just in time to see Abe fall from his horse. An icy hand closed about Radley's heart. Leaving the return fire to Dudley, he hurried to his son's side.

"Where you hurt, boy?"

"My arm. It ain't so bad, Pa."

Rad examined the wound quickly and breathed a sigh of relief. As the youngster had said, it wasn't serious.

"Mount up," he told his boy. "We're getting out of here. We got more important business in Red Gap."

As he spoke, he hauled his boy onto his feet and boosted him into his saddle. Once he was certain Abe was able to handle the reins, Radley vaulted up into his own saddle and flung his horse around. Shouting to Dudley and Link to haul ass, he clapped spurs to his horse and raced from the compound, Abe following. At once Link and Dudley mounted up and followed after them at full gallop.

Matt was aware of a miserable pounding in his head. He clenched his teeth and sat up. At first he thought he had maybe lost his left eye, since he could see nothing out of it but a blazing red haze. Then he put his hand up to the eye and found that it was intact, but covered with blood. His fingers followed the path of the blood and found that the round had seared a neat furrow the length of his skull, just above his temple. But he was lucky. The bullet had not broken through his skull.

Not that that made it hurt any less. It felt as if someone had branded him on the head with a red-hot iron.

He groaned and tried to stand up. Running footsteps caused him to look around. He saw Parsons and Vinegar Bill running toward him from the bunkhouse. Gritting his teeth, he pushed himself up onto his feet.

"I'm all right," he told Parsons, the first one to reach him. "What about the others?"

Then he saw the sprawled body of Bo Allen. One glance told him the man was dead. He felt sick. He had liked Bo.

"Help me get into the house," he told his two hands. "I need to wash off this blood and clean myself up."

His head spun sickeningly as he started up the veranda steps. Parsons kept close beside him, ready to help if he was needed.

But he made it into the ranch house on his own and shuffled over to the sink. Putting his head under the pump, he told Parsons to drown him. As the icy water sluiced over his aching head, he felt better almost at once.

He heard Gramps and Bull hurrying into the house, and a moment later his grandfather had sat him down and was wrapping a fresh bandage of torn bedsheets around his skull. While the old man worked, Bull asked if Matt was still going into Red Gap.

Matt squinted at his foreman. "I expect this here wound will delay me some, Bull, but it sure as hell won't stop me. If that deputy marshal and his crazy Indian need another gun to go against Rad, he has it."

Bull cleared his throat. "I want to make that party too, Matt. I liked Bo."

"I'd rather have you stay here to guard the place. Rad might get back here somehow."

"Let him go with you," said Gramps, tugging expertly on the bandage. "We don't need no help to keep off that buzzard. Why, me an' Vinegar Bill an' Parsons'll ventilate him good and proper if he shows his ugly face around here again. You don't need to worry none about us, Matt."

Matt smiled at Gramps, then winced from the pain it caused.

Through narrow, painful eyes he looked carefully at Bull. "All right. Come ahead, Bull." Still squinting, he said to

Parsons, "Bury Bo while I'm gone, will you? In the plot back of the house, near where my wife's buried. And make a box for him."

"We'll take care of it, Matt."

Chapter 11

Later that same day, around sundown, Longarm was sitting at a table in the Red Gap with Pete Geller when Roland Smith, flanked by two of his teamsters, approached his table. When they reached it, they did not offer to sit down, and Longarm did not invite them to. The saloon had grown ominously quiet the moment Smitty and his two companions entered. Now there was not a man in it who was not watching.

And Longarm did not blame them. The big man had not grown any smaller since they last met. His shoulders were still a match for any grizzly, and his arms still compared favorably with telegraph poles. But his black bush of a beard had, if anything, grown a mite wilder, and the eyes now peering out from behind it at Longarm seemed a lot more wary.

And deadly.

"Welcome back to Red Gap, Longarm," the big man said, his voice deceptively gentle.

"Thanks, Smitty."

"Heard you was lookin' for me."

"That's right," Longarm replied. "Thanks for coming over here so promptly. When did you get in?"

"I didn't come so prompt," the man said. "I been in town since yesterday. Now what's this all about? Marge said you wanted to see me."

"I'll tell you what, Smitty. Why don't your two friends sit down here and have a drink on me with Pete. Then maybe you and I can find a quiet table where we can talk in private."

The big man considered this a moment, then shrugged. "Just so's it don't take all night. I got business, Longarm."

"It won't, I promise you," Longarm said, picking up his glass of rye and moving ahead of Smitty over to an empty table in the corner.

As he sat down across from Smitty, he glanced quickly about the saloon and saw that most of its patrons had lost interest the moment it became obvious that he and Smitty were not going to square off.

"First things first," said Longarm, waving a girl over to the table. "What are you drinking, Smitty?"

"Whiskey," the man replied.

Longarm told the girl. She left. Longarm turned back to Smitty. "What I want to know, Smitty, is why you sent one of your men out to kill me."

Smitty appeared genuinely surprised by Longarm's question. "Hey, now, Longarm, what are you trying to pull here? I never sent no one after you—and that's the truth." He smiled then and leaned back in his chair. "If I *had* sent someone after you, you wouldn't be sittin' across from me now."

The girl brought Smitty's drink. He threw it down without hesitation, looked up at her, and said, "Bring a bottle, Janie. Longarm's buyin'." As the girl left for the bottle, he looked back at Longarm.

"You say someone tried to bushwhack you?"

"That's right, Smitty."

"And when did this happen?"

"Three days ago."

"Where?"

"Beaver Pass."

146

"And you say it was one of my men."

"It was."

"Who?"

"Hale Murdock."

Smitty straightened. "So that's where the son of a bitch disappeared to. Now ain't that interestin'."

The girl brought him the bottle and looked at Longarm. Longarm paid her, then glanced back at Smitty. "You say Murdock just disappeared. You had no idea he was after me, and you had nothing to do with his leaving?"

"That's what I said," Smitty replied, filling his shot glass.

"You're telling me Murdock just up and left. Out of a clear blue sky, he just up and decided to take after me. He was bored, maybe."

"I didn't say that." Smitty was enjoying himself. He smiled across the table at Longarm, downed the contents of the shot glass, then wiped his mouth with the back of his hand. "No, sir. I didn't say that at all. You might say he left under mysterious circumstances."

"And just when was this?" Longarm asked patiently.

"A couple of days before you say he tried to kill you."

"Mysterious circumstances, you said. What were they, Smitty?"

"Of course, it was just something I heard, you understand." He leaned back and smiled, obviously enjoying Longarm's puzzlement.

"Let's have it, Smitty."

"Supposin' I don't want to tell you. After all, Murdock was one of my men."

"Not anymore, he ain't. He's dead."

"I figured that."

"And maybe you can also figure that I'm not about to sit here forever while you play cat-and-mouse with me, Smitty. Someone tried to murder me, and if you know why and don't tell me, I'll have to consider that a *very* unfriendly act."

"You think that makes me upset, Longarm?"

For the first time Longarm caught the menacing anger in Smitty's voice. He was holding something back, something that was eating at him. Longarm decided he would have to dig that out if he was going to get any cooperation from the teamster.

"All right, Smitty. Out with it. What's eatin' on you? Something's bothering you, and it ain't the fact that Murdock ran off to bushwhack me."

"You're right, Longarm. It ain't."

"So what is it?"

"Heard you spent some time with my woman last time you was here. I don't like you messin' with Marge Pennock, Longarm."

"I wasn't aware she was your woman, Smitty. I didn't see any tag around her neck that said she was your property and that I shouldn't touch. I figured it was her choice to make and I let her make it."

"Damn you! You mess with her again, and I'll break you in two with my bare hands."

"Careful you don't start making promises you can't keep, Smitty," Longarm drawled, leaning back in his seat.

Smitty studied Longarm for a moment, making a conscious effort to control himself. "All right," he said at length. "Best we let that pass for now. No sense in getting our bowels in an uproar over a cheap goddamn whore."

Longarm saw that Smitty was trying to rile him—and did his best to ignore his reference to Marge as a whore. "Good idea, Smitty," he said. "Now suppose we get back to Murdock. Why did he take after me with a Winchester?"

"Is that what he used?" Smitty remarked, suddenly amused. "Hell, he never was much of a shot with a rifle. 'Course, he always fancied he was good enough to pluck the ticks off a mule's back."

"That's what he used. A Winchester. And you're right. He was not that good a shot. Now if you keep dancing around the bush, Smitty, I'll just have to conclude that you put Murdock up to killing me. And then I'd be forced to act accordingly."

"You serious, Deputy?"

"I'm serious."

Smitty leaned forward. From the look in his eyes it was clear to Longarm that the cat-and-mouse game was over. "All right, damn you. It wasn't me that sicked him on you.

Murdock met himself a damn pretty-lookin' Mex, right in here, Longarm. She sweet-talked him, passed some gold to the poor son of a bitch, and the next morning he lit out."

Longarm reached across the table for the whiskey bottle, filled his glass, then leaned back to consider what Smitty had just told him, confident that he had succeeded in goading the man into telling the truth.

A pretty-looking Mex. A woman. And then he remembered something that had been nagging at the back of his mind for days. *Longman.* That was what Murdock had called him when Longarm had asked who he was and why he was trying to kill him.

Your executioner, Longman, Murdock had replied.

And that was what Rosita Sanchez had called him that morning he awoke to find her standing at the foot of his bed, pointing a Colt Peacemaker at him: *Longman.*

Rosita Sanchez. She had followed him all the way up here and given Hale Murdock those gold coins to bushwhack him. Deputy Marshal Wallace, it seemed, had not been able to find her. Or if he had, he had been unable to convince her that Longarm had not meant to shoot her father, that her father had forced the issue when he had come at Longarm with a case knife. She was still lusting after her vengeance.

It was his own fault. He had told Billy Vail not to hold her.

"Thanks, Smitty. It all comes together now. Which lets you off the hook. I know who that woman was who sent Murdock after me. Does she still come in here?"

"Nope." Smitty seemed a trifle disappointed with himself for saying as much as he had. "She . . . rode out of here a few days ago. Guess maybe she got tired of waiting for Murdock to come back. Good thing she didn't stay. She'd of had a heart attack, watchin' you and that blamed Indian trail in here this afternoon."

"While she was here, Smitty, where did she stay?"

"The hotel."

"Then Marge must have met her."

"I reckon."

"But you say this Mexican woman is gone now."

149

"Dammit! You callin' me a liar?"

Longarm didn't answer the teamster. He wasn't calling him a liar to his face. No sense in that. But Longarm had little reason to believe Smitty. He had caught an evasiveness in his manner the moment he asked him if Rosita was still in Red Gap. And that meant there was a good chance that Rosita Sanchez was still at the hotel.

Longarm took a deep breath. Faith Cameron and her four children were rooming at the hotel, as well. For a moment he felt panic, then calmed himself down. Rosita Sanchez was after *him,* not a woman and her children whom he might have befriended.

Still, with a woman that filled with venom, that crazed with the desire for vengeance, how could he be sure? He caught Pete's eye and beckoned him over to his table.

"Pete," he said, as soon as the man got there, "I want you to go back to the hotel and check on Faith and the kids. See that there isn't anything they need. And then stay with them. You understand?"

"Sure, Longarm. But—what's this all about? Is anything wrong?"

"Do as I say, Pete. I'll explain later. It may be nothing at all. Just keep your eyes open, that's all."

With a brisk nod, Pete turned and hurried from the saloon.

Longarm looked back at Smitty. It was obvious to him that Smitty was shielding Rosita. And for the same reason Hale Murdock had come after him with a Winchester. More of those freshly minted gold coins.

But that would have to wait. Longarm had one more important matter to settle with Smitty.

"Have some more whiskey, Smitty. Like you said, it's on me."

The big man looked warily at Longarm as he took back the whiskey bottle.

"Smitty," Longarm began carefully, "I'd like to talk about those four murdered Treasury agents, the ones that washed up close by Taylor's Ferry."

"What about them?" he asked, throwing a fresh shot of whiskey down his throat.

"I been thinking. There was no reason for Rad or the

150

MacLaggans to work that hard to bring those bodies all the way down there and dump them in the Snake. Makes no sense, if you think about it. The last thing any of them would want to do is kill an agent and then advertise it. Works best all around if the poor sons of bitches just ride off into yonder mountains looking for moonshine and disappear."

"Guess so. What's your point?"

"The question is, Smitty, what's *your* point? Why did you do it? Why did you go to the trouble of hauling those dead bastards all the way down to the Snake so you could dump them? You're in this moonshine business with Rad and MacLaggan. You're bootlegging their liquor, then returning with the mail. And that makes you the only one around who had the opportunity to mutilate, then dump those four revenuers."

"That's crazy, Longarm. Why the hell would I want to do a fool thing like that?"

"That's what I'm asking. Why?"

"I didn't do no such a thing, Longarm. Indians done it, I told you. Shoshone."

"That's what you want everyone to believe. But Shoshone don't mutilate bodies the way those agents were mutilated. Cheyenne do, maybe. But not Shoshone. Someone familiar with Cheyenne ways could have made those mutilations, though. Didn't you say you fought the Cheyenne before you started packing the mail?"

"I'm tellin' you, Longarm, I didn't have nothing to do with them killings. And you can't prove I did, neither."

"Maybe I can't, Smitty. But it sure as hell wasn't the Shoshone. I didn't see a single Shoshone while I was up in those mountains messin' with your moonshining friends."

"What about Frank Fools Crow? He likes to use a knife now and then."

"He's a Sioux—or part Sioux. And he didn't do it."

"You're a goddamn Indian-lover!"

Longarm took the accusation calmly, though almost every head in the saloon turned in their direction when they heard Smitty's shout. Shrugging, Longarm replied, "I've met some I've liked, yes. And some I've hated as much as

I've hated any white man. Depends on how a man behaves, Smitty."

Getting to his feet abruptly, Longarm threw a tip on the table for the girl who had served them. "Thanks for coming in to see me, Smitty."

Then he turned and strode from the saloon.

Dusk had fallen by the time Longarm emerged from the saloon. He was anxious to return to the hotel to check with Marge on Rosita Sanchez, but decided instead to visit the doctor's office first to check on Frank Fools Crow's condition. He was halfway across when he heard a commotion and looked up the street to see Black Elk and Sits Tall Woman riding into Red Gap.

He crossed the street, then waited for them in front of the barbershop. When they saw him, they put their mounts in at the hitch rail in front of the barbershop and dismounted. A crowd had gathered by this time.

"Where is Fools Crow?" Black Elk asked.

"Upstairs. With the doctor."

"He is hurt bad?" Sits Tall Woman asked.

"He took a slug in the chest. But the doc got it out, and it looks like he's going to be all right."

"We have come to take him out of this place," Black Elk announced.

"That's fine, Black Elk, but you'll have to wait until he's strong enough to travel."

Black Elk looked at Sits Tall Woman. She was the one to speak next. "We want to see Fools Crow."

"Follow me," Longarm said, starting up the steps leading to Doctor Ramsdell's office.

A moment later, Fools Crow was frowning sternly up at his two younger siblings. "You return from Sitting Bull already?" he demanded.

"We heard you were hurt."

"How the hell did you hear that?" Longarm asked, astonished. "It only happened last night."

Black Elk smiled at Longarm, then down at his brother. "We heard."

"You did not go far," said Fools Crow, his voice weak but accusing. "You said you would go north into mountains—away from here."

"We change our minds," said Sits Tall Woman. "Now we take you away from here. From now on, we stay together. Sitting Bull will soon return, and the white man's medicine will fail against him. We will wait in the mountains together for that day."

Frank Fools Crow looked at Longarm, his eyes only showing the amusement—and warmth—these two had brought him. "I do not think that day will come soon, Longarm. But it will be a good thing to await such a day with these two."

"I'll leave you now," said Longarm. "I have business at the hotel."

The Indian nodded.

"How's he doing?" Longarm asked the doctor as soon as he reached the outer office.

Before replying, the doctor filled a glass from a jug standing on his desk, then took out another glass for Longarm. Longarm stopped him with a wave of his hand. The doctor shrugged and, with a few quick swallows, drank half the glass he had filled. Then he wiped his mouth, coughed, and looked at Longarm with bright, feverish eyes.

"He is a strong man. He will survive. I am sure of it."

"That was a nice job you did, Doc. I saw how far you had to go in for that bullet. Nine out of ten doctors would have botched it."

"Yes. And even if they had retrieved the bullet, the patient would have died of a raging fever, one that would soon have burned the life out of him."

"I know it, Doc. You're good. So what the hell are you doing in this place? In Red Gap?"

"I came West to study the Indian medicine men, the *pejuta wicasa*. I had the foolish notion that perhaps they would have a cure for what ails me."

"And what's that, Doc?"

"The great curse of civilization, Deputy. Consumption. My entire family succumbed to its ravages. I am the last

153

survivor, if you can call me that."

"You might live a mite longer if you'd go easy on that moonshine."

"Ah, yes, But what would be the sense of living a bit longer, Deputy?"

"You've given up, have you?"

"Let us say I have come to terms with my condition."

"Before you do that, I suggest you talk to that Indian in there. He's a pretty damn smart medicine man, from what I can figure." Longarm took off his hat and leaned closer to the doctor. "Take a look at my scalp. He brought me through a fever and then sewed me up as good as new. He's a medicine man, Doc. The real article."

The doctor's eyebrows lifted as he inspected Longarm's wound. "It is a fine job he did, indeed," he said. "I doubt that there will be the slightest scar."

With a thoughtful frown, the man sat back down in his chair. "No, Deputy. This Indian's medicine cannot cure me. Indeed, consumption has already begun to stalk through these aborigines. It would be better for me if I stayed away from him."

"Maybe you're right, Doc," Longarm said wearily. "But do me a favor, will you? Go easy on that firewater, will you—and keep a sharp eye on that Indian for me. And his brother and sister."

"Very well," said the doctor, reluctantly stoppering his jug and placing it back in his drawer.

"Thanks, Doc," Longarm said, starting for the door. "When this is all over, maybe I'll buy you a bottle of genuine booze."

"I'd appreciate that, Deputy."

With a nod, Longarm left the doctor's office.

It was dark when Longarm reached the hotel. Sitting on the veranda were Pete Geller and Faith Cameron. They were talking softly and did not notice his approach until he was within a few feet of the veranda steps.

"Longarm," Faith called to him softly, "is everything all right?"

154

"As long as Pete's here, keeping an eye on you. How're the children?"

"They are asleep, just. Pete helped me put them to bed. We've only been out here a few minutes."

"All right. Pete, take your mattress and place it outside Faith's door tonight."

"You going to explain what's up?" the man asked, exasperated.

"I'm not sure myself, Pete. Please, just do as I say."

With a sigh, Pete said, "All right, Mr. Long."

Longarm bade both of them good night and continued on into the hotel, where he found Marge's assistant at the front desk. He was a very young man who was trying desperately to grow a mustache. Longarm asked him where the postmistress was, and he told Longarm he thought she was in her room.

"Which room would that be?"

"Room ten. Down the hall, Mr. Long."

Longarm nodded and proceeded down the narrow passageway, paused before Marge's door, and knocked. There was no response. He knocked again, louder.

Longarm thought he heard the rustle of a dress close by the door. And then, in a whisper that was barely audible, Longarm heard, "Who's there?"

"Longarm."

"Oh, Longarm," Marge whispered. "You mustn't be seen here—by my door!"

"I'd like to speak to you, Marge."

"Go to your room. I'll find a way to get up there."

"How soon?"

"As soon as I can. Please, Longarm."

"All right."

Longarm moved back down the hall to the small lobby. He saw the desk clerk watching him. "She's not in her room," Longarm told him.

"Shall I leave a message for her?"

"Never mind," Longarm replied, moving up the stairs to his room.

Longarm waited in his room without lighting his lamp.

Lying on his back in the darkness, he heard Faith and Pete mounting the stairs to the third floor. Not long after, he heard the man dragging his mattress along the corridor so that he could take his vigil outside Faith's room.

It was probably a needless precaution, but that woman had suffered enough, and Longarm did not intend to take any chances.

At last he heard soft footsteps approaching his door. A key was thrust into his lock. The door opened. A woman entered, then closed the door. Longarm became aware of her pale face peering at him.

Longarm sat up, his revolver cocked and aimed at the dim figure standing by his door. "Is that you, Marge?"

"No!" came the hissed response.

And with it the awesome, thunderous detonation of a Colt revolver. But Longarm had already flung himself off the bed. He struck the floor on his back and managed to get off a return shot. Through the coils of smoke that now choked the room, he saw Rosita duck aside, raise her gun, and fire again. The slug whined off the iron bedstead. Longarm crabbed to the far corner, turned, and saw Rosita outlined for an instant against the bed's white sheets.

He should have fired then. But he hesitated. Rosita fired at him a third time. The floor in front of Longarm splintered. Tiny shards of wood struck his face. He returned Rosita's fire.

She cried out, then slumped. For a moment she hung over the bed, then rolled off it to the floor. The sound of her soft body striking the floor almost made Longarm sick.

The door was kicked open. Longarm saw—in the light from the hall lamp—Smitty's oversized figure looming in the doorway.

"Rosita!" he cried.

She moaned. Smitty dashed into the room.

"Hold it right there," said Longarm, getting to his feet.

Smitty whirled and fired, shattering the window beside Longarm. The lawman flung himself to one side, returning the teamster's fire as he did so. His bullet caught Smitty— Longarm saw the man's dark figure rock back. But the big teamster was all but unstoppable. Reaching down, he

156

grabbed Rosita, flung her over his shoulder, and bolted from the room.

Longarm waited until Smitty's heavy footsteps on the stairs faded. A moment later he heard the hotel door slam open and the man's heavy tread on the porch steps. Only then did he walk slowly over to his bed and light the lamp on his bureau. Next he righted the nightstand, placed the lantern on it, and sat wearily on the edge of his bed. When he glanced down and saw Rosita's blood, he moved away from it.

He could have fired upon Smitty when the man started from the room with the wounded woman, but enough was enough. He didn't have the heart for it. And he knew from experience he would regret that lapse.

Pete appeared in the open doorway, his gun out. "My God, Mr. Long," he said, stepping cautiously into the room. "What happened?"

"I been shot at."

"Who did it?"

"A crazy woman and Smitty."

Pete stopped before Longarm. "What'd you say, Mr. Long?"

"Never mind," Longarm said wearily. "Go back upstairs. I'll handle this."

Pete hesitated, then shrugged and holstered his weapon. "I would've got here sooner," he said, "but I wanted to check to make sure Mrs. Cameron and her kids were all right."

"You did the right thing. Now do as I say. Go on back upstairs and keep an eye out."

A few moments after Pete left, Marge appeared in the doorway, tears streaming down her face. "I heard your voice—talking to that Pete fellow."

"That ain't no reason to cry, Marge."

"I...thought you were dead. That Smitty—or that woman—had killed you."

"Come on in and close the door, Marge," Longarm said. "I've been waiting for you."

She closed the door swiftly, then flung herself into his arms. He comforted her as best he could, then gently sat her down in a chair alongside his bed.

"You didn't need to worry," he told her, sitting back on the bed and watching her. "I knew you were not alone in your room. But I didn't expect Rosita. I expected someone else."

"Smitty?"

"That's right."

"You could have been killed." She wept softly. "I should have tried to warn you."

"Forget it, Marge."

"Smitty turned on me. He made me do it, Longarm. He's thrown in with her!"

"I figured that, too. But why did he let her go after me alone?"

"He didn't have anything to do with that. He was gone. It was her idea, as soon as she knew you were alone, waiting for me. When Smitty came in, she was already up here. That's when the shooting began."

"And now she's hurt—and hurt bad. Dead, maybe. That fool woman!"

"Smitty beat me, Longarm," she wept. "You should see my body. What he done to it."

"Marge," he said, ignoring her bid for his sympathy, "why did Smitty dump those mutilated bodies in the Snake?"

She left her chair and sat beside him on the bed, weeping softly. "Hold me, Longarm. Please," she said. "I feel so awful."

He let her rest her head on his shoulder, and put his arms around her and held her closely. Gradually the tension in her body relaxed. She stopped crying. Then she turned her face to his, inviting a kiss.

Longarm kissed her.

"You won't like me if I tell you about those bodies, Longarm."

"Try me."

"It was Smitty's idea. We're in partnership, Longarm. And we've loaned out lots of money to settlers and store-keepers in the town. If we could put this town on the map, we'd be in charge. We'd have control."

"But tucked away up here in the mountains, the world

was passing you by."

"Yes, Longarm. That's it." She brightened at once. "Oh, I knew you'd understand."

"So you needed publicity. Big doings in Red Gap. The army called in to put down a Shoshone uprising. And with the army, you hoped, would come a stagecoach line—or better yet, a railroad—and then, prosperity."

"Yes, that's it, Longarm."

"So Smitty brought the corpses of those Treasury agents down with him on one of his trips. And dumped them."

"Yes."

"Did he kill them?"

She hesitated only a moment. "Yes."

"And mutilate them?"

She shuddered. "He said that would attract the army for sure. They'd think it was the Shoshone that done it."

She pulled away from him. "You hate me, don't you?"

"I don't hate you, Marge. But it is difficult for me to understand how you could throw in with a man like Smitty."

She closed her eyes. "I'm a woman, Longarm. A lonely woman. I'm strong, up to a point. A big man like Smitty— well, he has an attraction for a woman alone up here, without anyone. Surely you can understand that."

"Yes, I can understand that."

She got to her feet and turned to face him. "You're strong too, Longarm. That's why I've turned to you. Why I told Smitty I didn't want to have anything more to do with him. That's why he beat me. That's why he left me for Rosita."

A shot from below in the street shattered what glass was left in the window. Longarm yanked Marge to the floor, then blew out the lamp. Unholstering his .44, he flattened himself against the wall next to the window.

"Longarm!" Smitty called from the street. The big man's wound was obviously not slowing him down much. "You still up there?"

"I'm here!"

"Rosita Sanchez is dead. You killed her in cold blood. Me and my men are going to make you pay for that. And we're going to have help doing it."

"You'll need it, Smitty."

"I just got word. Radley is on his way. He'll be here in the morning—and you won't be gettin' no help from them ranchers, neither. Rad took care of them hisself."

To punctuate his words, Smitty fired again, catching enough unbroken windowpane to send a small explosion of glass shards across the room.

Longarm waited, but there was no more shooting. Cautiously he looked down at the street. Smitty was gone. He was going to wait for Radley to show up.

Smitty wanted a sure thing, it seemed.

Chapter 12

Longarm turned away from the window. Marge was just getting up off the floor where he had flung her. In the darkened room, he could see clearly her wide, frightened eyes as she pushed her hair off her forehead and stared fearfully at him.

"What are you going to do?" she asked. "He'll kill you. I know that man. Once he gets it in his mind to do something—"

"Go back to your room, Marge," he told her. "Lock your door and stay there until this is over."

She moistened her dry lips. "You don't want me . . . for anything?"

"No, Marge. Not now. But I might have some questions later, if you don't mind."

She nodded furtively then, and he read what she was thinking: *If you survive, Longarm.* Then, no longer moving like a woman bereft, she slipped like a cat from his room. When the sound of her swift, light feet on the stairs had faded completely, he holstered his .44 and walked over to the corner of the room where he'd left the Winchester that Faith Cameron had given him.

He'd lost his own Winchester along with his horse at the Robinsons' place, but Faith Cameron had insisted he replace it with her dead husband's weapon. He brought it with him as he moved cautiously to the door and pulled it open. He was about to move out of the room when he heard someone rush into the hotel, head for the stairs, and then race up them. Holding his rifle held at the ready just in case, Longarm waited.

Will, the Camerons' hired hand, appeared before him, his face streaming with perspiration. "What's the hurry, Will?"

"I was in the saloon," he said. "I heard what they're plannin', Long."

"I'd take it kindly, Will, if you'd go nice and slow and tell me just what you heard. Nothing like knowing what's in the other player's hand when bluffin' time comes." Longarm pulled the door open wider. "Get in here."

Will ducked swiftly into the room. Longarm closed the door behind him.

"Now let's have it. What did you hear?"

"Smitty's warned the townies to stay out of it. And there ain't no one goin' against him, as far as I can see. Until this is over, one way or the other, the stores are all staying closed and anyone on the streets is liable to get his head blowed off. It's just going to be him and Rad against us, Longarm."

"Thanks for including yourself in with me, Will. But that ain't the way I'm figurin' it."

Will swallowed. It was obvious he was relieved. "Anyway, Smitty ain't goin' to have all his teamsters backin' him. Only three of them are in this with him. And Jack Sharpe, the dealer at the Red Gap."

"What's he got against me?"

"Nothin'. He's just pretty tight with Smitty."

"So that's five—until Rad gets here."

Will nodded, his eyes feverish with excitement. "What you goin' to do, Longarm?"

"Think I'll move out now and see if I can lower the odds some."

162

"Right now? While it's still dark?"

"Can't see any advantage in waiting until Rad gets here with his bunch. The darkness makes a good ally when the odds are against you. What about that MacLaggan crew?"

"I heard they pulled out of this when they found out what Rad had done to the Camerons."

"That's a help. Where's Smitty and his men now?"

"They're drinkin' courage in the Red Gap."

"Has Bo Allen returned yet?"

"Nope."

Longarm shook his head, troubled. He felt sudden concern for Bo. "Smitty just got through advertising that I couldn't count on any help from the other ranchers. Said Rad had seen to it. I don't like the sound of that. I hope Bo is all right."

"Where's Pete?" Will asked.

"Upstairs, outside Faith Cameron's door. I was thinkin' maybe you'd better join him up there. If I begin to get on Smitty's nerves, he might try to get at me through Mrs. Cameron or her children."

"You think he'd do a thing like that?"

"I wouldn't put it past him."

"I'll stay on this landing, then. Anyone comes up those stairs will have to deal with me."

"Good idea, Will," Longarm said, heading for the door.

Watching him go, Will moistened his dry lips and said, "Good luck, Mr. Long."

"Thanks." Longarm opened the door and stepped out into the hallway. Glancing back in at the shadowy figure of Will, he said, "Soon's I'm gone, you go up there and tell Pete you're down here."

Longarm moved down the stairs to the lobby, past a very nervous-looking desk clerk, and down the narrow hallway. He saw a light under Marge's door, kept going, and let himself into the alley.

He kept to it until he was in back of the Red Gap. He could hear Smitty and his army inside, their voices heavy with liquor. From the way their voices echoed, it was obvious they were now the saloon's sole patrons. The Red

163

Gap had a small back porch. Longarm mounted it, then nudged the rear door with the barrel of his Winchester. It opened without protest.

Longarm stepped inside and found himself in a well-worn passageway—the one that led to the outhouses in back. A single lantern burned fitfully on a wall shelf. From where he was standing, Longarm could see only one end of the bar and little else. The barkeep was out of sight, as were Smitty and the others.

His tall frame moving with the lightness of a cat, Longarm made it to the end of the narrow hallway and peered carefully around the corner into the saloon. The very bored barkeep was leaning wearily on the bar as he listened to Smitty and his men regale each other with how they were going to wipe the street up with that damn fool of a deputy U.S. marshal. Smitty was sitting at a table near the wall opposite the bar, his back to Longarm; three others were at the table with them. They were trying to play poker, but seemed to be having trouble concentrating as they traded gibes and tossed down drinks. Longarm counted them again. Four in all.

Will had said there were five.

That was when he heard the creak of a board behind him. He whirled around to find himself looking into Rosita's furious face. She had just come out of a room off the hallway. He could see the open door behind her. Rosita was not dead after all, it appeared, though her right arm was in a sling. She was holding the poker over her head with her left hand.

And that was undoubtedly why it did not land squarely on Longarm's head as it was meant to, but glanced off the wall instead, then slammed crookedly down on Longarm's left shoulder. Wincing in pain, he managed to twist the poker out of Rosita's hand. Cringing away from him, Rosita bolted back into her room.

Longarm heard the cries of Smitty and the others behind him as they jumped up from the table and started toward him. Dropping the poker, Longarm spun around and lifted his Winchester. Aiming deliberately high, he squeezed off a shot. The four men scrambled hastily to a halt. He had them flat-footed. Yet something was wrong. Not one of them seemed at all perturbed that Longarm had the drop on them.

And Smitty just stood there, grinning. Longarm could see where his bullet had caught him earlier—on the forearm, just below the elbow. A dirty, bloodstained bandage was wrapped around it. It didn't seem to be bothering him in the slightest.

"Come on in and talk this over, Longarm," Smitty said. "No call for us to do any more shootin'."

As he spoke, he backed up, the others moving along with him. Longarm knew the man had something up his sleeve as he stepped toward him. But what? And then he remembered again the missing man.

He halted. There was a movement off to his right. He did not take the time to look in that direction as he flung himself backward into the hallway. A sawed-off shotgun crashed thunderously, but its blast just missed him—shredding the woodwork on the other side of the hallway instead.

Longarm raced on down the passage and out of the saloon. Leaping from the porch, he headed for the nearest outhouse. He was ducking behind one corner of it when one of Smitty's men rushed out after him, another one following on his heels.

Longarm fired on the first. He caught him low and brought him to his knees. The other ducked to one side and disappeared into the night. Longarm waited a moment, hoping Smitty would make an appearance. But the big teamster was too smart for that.

Longarm took off up the alley after the second man. Two blocks farther down he caught sight of a shadow darting around a corner, heading for the street, and took after it. He was almost to the street when he sensed danger and pulled up, then dove into the shadows—just in time. The night ahead of him exploded with an orange flash and a round zinged past him. The fellow he was chasing had been waiting at the corner of the building.

Longarm groaned and slid noisily to the ground. There was an empty bottle by his foot. He kicked it against the wall, then groaned again. Lying on his back, his colt in his hand, he waited as his would-be assassin crept nervously toward him, his sixgun gleaming blue in the dim light. Within four feet of Longarm's still body, he paused warily.

Longarm groaned a third time. Convinced that Longarm was hurt badly, the fellow took courage and edged still closer. Longarm could hear his heavy breathing. It was fast, like the panting of an animal. Again the teamster paused. This time he raised his weapon and cocked it. The double metallic click filled the alley.

Longarm fired up at the figure looming over him. The force of the .44-40 slug flung the man back, but he did not go down. Longarm rolled over swiftly, crabbed to his left, and fired up at the man a second time. With a faint cry, the teamster collapsed forward onto the ground, hugging his midsection with both arms.

Snatching up his rifle, Longarm holstered his .44 and darted back the way he had come. In a moment he was at the rear of the saloon once more. The man he had shot earlier was lying facedown in the alley, his gun a couple of feet from his lifeless, outstretched hand. Longarm kicked the weapon into the night, then cautiously mounted the back porch. The gunfire out in front, more than two blocks away, should have drawn Smitty and his two remaining cohorts out of the saloon.

That was his hope, anyway, as he moved softly through the doorway. Reaching the room where Rosita had been hidden earlier, he saw a light under the door, nudged it open, and stepped inside. A lamp was guttering fitfully on a small table by the bed. Rosita was still in the room. She was on the bed, lying on her back, her magnificent corona of gleaming black hair framing her pale face.

And staring up at him out of that pale face Longarm saw the glassy, unblinking eyes of a dead woman.

Looking closer, Longarm saw that the side of her skull had been smashed in—more than likely by the barrel of Smitty's sixgun. If this shootout didn't go the way he wanted, Smitty had planned on cutting out—but not without this foolish dead woman's fortune in gold.

Longarm froze. Someone was in the hall outside.

He flung himself back against the wall as a tall, lean figure carrying a sawed-off shotgun barged into the room, both barrels erupting. The sound in the tiny room was deafening—so loud, in fact, that the fellow probably did not hear the report of Longarm's Colt as it blasted a hole in his back.

Longarm bent down and rolled the fellow over. It was the dealer, Jack Sharpe. He was still alive, but just barely. Longarm straightened, left the dying gambler, and hurried from the saloon. He was suddenly anxious to return to the hotel. The sight of Rosita's dead body had shown him what Smitty's next move was likely to be. Longarm broke into a run and cursed. Already, he realized, he might be too late.

No, he was not too late.

Two saddled horses were waiting at the rear of the hotel. As he pounded closer, however, he saw a shadowy figure dart between him and the horses. At once Longarm flung himself to one side. The figure ducked behind a rain barrel and fired at Longarm, who flung himself instantly to one side, levering the Winchester swiftly, sending a devastatingly rapid fire into the barrel.

He heard the rounds slamming into the barrel. Three or four streams of water gleamed in the moonlight. Then came a cry. The man behind the barrel came upright, then spun around. Longarm threw himself flat, his rifle trained on the wounded man. His trigger finger was tightening when the man sagged forward over the barrel. Knocking it over, he lay facedown in what little rain water still trickled out.

That made four. One more to go. Smitty.

Longarm scrambled to his feet and raced on toward the hotel. He was still a block away when he saw the two figures hurry from the hotel, mount up, and lash their horses to a sudden gallop. One of the riders was Smitty; there was no mistaking his bulky figure. And the rider with him was Marge Pennock.

Longarm stopped, lifted his rifle, and fired at Smitty as the big man leaned over his horse's neck, urging it on. Longarm thought he saw Smitty slump forward for an instant, but he couldn't be sure in the darkness. He fired a second time, hopelessly.

The horses cut down the next alley. He raced after them and reached the street in time to see them vanish into the darkness. A moment later he heard the sudden clatter as their horses pounded over the wooden bridge.

For a moment Longarm stood in the street, the moonlight flooding over his lone figure. He could feel the townspeople's eyes on him as they peered out from behind darkened windows. At last, certain that it was over, they began scurrying out of their holes. The sound of heavy footsteps running over the wooden walks filled the night with a dim thunder.

He heard running footsteps and turned to see Will and Pete dash out of the hotel and hurry down the steps toward him.

"You all right, Mr. Long?" Pete asked, pulling up beside him.

"I'm fine. How'd it go in there?"

"You were right," said Will, excitedly. "Smitty and one of his men tried to get up to Mrs. Cameron. But we waited until they could see our rifles poking down their snouts then told them to back off or we'd blow them to hell and gone."

Longarm smiled. "I suspicion they backed off."

Pete nodded grimly. "Smitty went back downstairs. I heard the other one go on out and race off."

"That was Smitty rode off just now, wasn't it?" asked Will. "The one you was shootin' at?"

"That's right."

"Who was that with him?"

"Marge Pennock, the postmistress."

"Jesus," said Pete. "That woman was in this with him all the time. That right?"

"Looks that way, don't it?"

Will looked around at the silent, moonlit street. "Is it over now? he asked nervously.

"If you mean did I get that other one with Smitty—the one that came up the stairs with him—the answer is yes.

But we been promised some more visitors to Red Gap come sunup, don't forget. Rad and his crew."

Pete nodded grimly. "Well, at least that gives us a breather."

"Pete, I suggest you go on back inside and look after Mrs. Cameron and her kids. More than likely she's wondering right now what the situation is. Will, I want you to come with me."

As Pete headed back into the hotel, Longarm trudged wearily across the street with Will. Shadowy figures watched them from doorways. A few townsmen had crowded into the Red Gap. Now they watched in silence from behind the batwings as Will and Longarm mounted the steps to the doctor's office and knocked.

The doctor pulled the door open.

"How's Fools Crow?" Longarm asked, as he stepped into the office with Will.

"That was close to being a major operation, Marshal. He's been sleeping fitfully ever since. But he has no fever and his color is good. He lost a considerable amount of blood before he got here. But as I said before, I am confident he will be all right." He smiled wanly, his death's head of a face becoming almost sinister. "If he doesn't get mixed up in a war, that is."

Longarm nodded wearily, then poked his head into the back room. Fools Crow was asleep, and Black Elk and Sits Tall Woman were sitting in opposite corners of the room. They were asleep also, he thought, until he saw Sits Tall Woman move her head slightly to look at him.

He beckoned to her. She rose immediately and followed Longarm back into the doctor's office. Longarm closed the door softly behind her.

"Will, here," he told her, "is going to help you and Black Elk take Frank Fools Crow out of Red Gap. Now. You'll have to act quickly. You'll be going with Mrs. Cameron and her kids." Longarm turned to Will. "Take the two wagons and head south as soon as you get across that bridge. Rad will be coming in from the north. As soon as daybreak comes, hole up somewhere and keep low. If I don't come

169

after you soon—or send someone—keep moving. It'll mean Rad owns this country, at least for a while."

Longarm looked at the doctor. "Can he be moved safely?"

"I don't suppose he has any alternative." The doctor looked at Sits Tall Woman. "You and Black Elk go easy with him."

The girl nodded.

Longarm turned to Will. "Get over to that livery and get those wagons, Will. I want all of you out of this town before the hour is out. That clear?"

Will nodded, slapped on his hat, and hurried from the office.

The sun had been up for close to an hour. Red Gap looked deserted. Not a single horse was switching its tail at a tie rail. There was no traffic. None of the places of business had opened. Even the saloon looked deserted. But that didn't mean a thing, Longarm realized. From behind every window eyes were peering, waiting for Radley to make his appearance.

Waiting for the *real* Wild West Show to begin.

Longarm was sitting in the rocker on the hotel porch, his Winchester across his lap, his hat back off his forehead to give him a better view of the street. He had just lit up his last cheroot and was smoking it carefully, savoring it. The more he thought about it, the more he realized how unlikely it was that he would ever give up smoking these cigars. A man had to have *some* bad habits.

Longarm did not expect Rad and his party to ride in across the bridge. They would more than likely dismount on the other side, then infiltrate the town. Longarm knew that by this time Rad had been apprised of the situation. He had seen a man ride out better than an hour before, heading north to warn Rad. It was one of Smitty's teamsters—the same one, Longarm figured, who had brought the news of Rad's coming the night before.

But Rad fooled Longarm. He came riding boldly across the bridge, his single companion the teamster who had ridden out to warn him.

Longarm levered a cartridge into the Winchester's chamber and waited. When Rad got to within easy talking distance of Longarm, he reined in, calmed his horse with a pat on its neck, then gazed coldly, appraisingly at the lawman.

"This is just between you and me, Long," he said. "And that Indian."

"He's gone."

"I know that. I'll tend to him later, don't you worry."

Longarm didn't reply.

"There ain't no sense in draggin' any more innocent people into this," Radley went on. "So why don't we just end this like gentlemen. Get down off that porch, and I'll dismount. We'll let Howie, here, tell us when."

"A duel between two gentlemen. Is that it?"

"That's right."

"You won't shoot until Howie gives the word."

"You have my word."

"Agreed."

Longarm got up, tossed his cheroot away regretfully, then descended the porch steps. At the same time, carefully and without haste, Radley dismounted. Howie reached down, took Radley's horse by the bridle, and led it out of the way, then released it and brought his own horse around so that he was facing the two of them.

Rad, like Longarm, held a rifle in his hands. A revolver was too untrustworthy at this distance. For serious killing, nothing was more effective than a rifle or a shotgun.

"I'll count to ten," said Howie, clearing his throat nervously.

"Hell," growled Radley. "Just tell us when!"

Howie never got to do that. Longarm heard a warning shout from his left, spun, and saw Doc Ramsdell on the landing outside his office, firing a Henry rifle down through the boards at a young fellow crouched beneath the steps. The kid's left arm was bandaged. In his right he held a shotgun. As Ramsdell continued to fire down on him, the young man bucked convulsively, then dropped his weapon and sprawled forward into the dust.

With a scream of rage, Radley forgot all about Longarm

171

and charged toward the stairway, levering his Winchester frantically as he sent a deadly fusillade up at the doctor. The skeletal figure on the landing staggered back from the impact of at least two bullets, dropped his weapon, then pitched headlong down the steps.

Longarm shouted at Radley, calling out to him to hold up.

Radley spun, his rifle at his waist still spitting death. Longarm flung himself to the ground, rolled over twice, then came up with his Winchester on his hip, firing. He caught Radley in the chest. Coughing blood, the man went down on one knee and levered another round into his Winchester. Longarm sent a second round into the man, catching him on the right side of his face, disintegrating it.

The man's head kicked back around, his torso following, the rifle detonating harmlessly into the air.

Longarm heard the pounding of hooves, spun around, and saw Dudley Withers riding full-tilt out from behind the hotel. He was riding with the reins in his teeth, a double-barreled shotgun at his hip. Longarm fired at the hard-charging rider, but his shot went wild. He started to run for cover, but Dudley swerved neatly and cut him off. Longarm changed direction as the horse's hooves pounded closer. Abruptly he threw himself to the ground, rolled over, and came up levering swiftly. He squeezed the trigger.

But there was only a click. He was out of ammunition. As he flung the rifle aside and clawed his Colt from its holster, he knew it was going to be too late. Dudley's horse loomed over him, the twin bores of his shotgun yawning like canyons. He saw Dudley's grinning face just behind them.

Two quick shots came from across the street. Dudley lurched sideways in his saddle. The shotgun's barrels hitched skyward a second before the weapon went off. A third shot knocked Dudley clean out of his saddle. He landed on his back, rolled over, then collapsed facedown in the dust. Longarm ducked his head as the riderless horse charged over him, its flying hooves clearing his head by inches.

Looking up from the ground, he glanced in the direction

172

from which the shots had come, and saw Matt Stokes and his foreman step into view from behind the barbershop, both men holding smoking revolvers.

And then once more came the sudden tattoo of hooves. Longarm whirled to see what looked like a Radley galloping out from behind the saloon, heading right for him. Sick by now of all this bloodshed, Longarm almost had to force himself to raise his .44. But when he saw that the rider did not carry a weapon in either hand, he quickly lowered his revolver.

"Hold your fire!" he called to Stokes and his foreman.

With a wailing sob, the rider dismounted, and flung himself into the dust beside Radley. He lifted the dead man's head onto his lap and began to cradle it. It was Radley's son, Longarm realized.

Slowly, with infinite weariness, Longarm looked away from the grieving son and crossed the street to thank Matt Stokes and his foreman. They had joined the party late, but better late than never.

Chapter 13

MacLaggan looked in astonishment at Longarm. As did everyone else at the table. For a moment MacLaggan thought that maybe Longarm was pulling his leg, that he had called him into Red Gap to make a fool of him.

But only for a moment. The look on Longarm's face dispelled that notion.

"Maybe I'm going too fast for you," said Longarm. "Let's eat this here apple one bite at a time."

"I'm listening," said MacLaggan.

"First off, you know I'm going to see to it that moonshining will not soon become profitable for you again. I have friends in the Treasury Department, and I don't want to be making this trip again. So that means you and the rest of those grangers up there have got to find a crop you can grow in this country—or pack up and move on."

"We tried corn. And we tried wheat."

"So, all I'm suggesting is you try potatoes."

"That's what I thought you said," MacLaggan replied, shaking his head.

They were all sitting around a table in the Red Gap hotel.

Faith entered with more coffee and a huge platter of doughnuts, which she placed down on the table before them.
MacLaggan's two boys almost broke their arms reaching
for them. Matt Stokes chuckled at their haste, but wasted
no time in reaching for a doughnut himself.

It was obvious to everyone that Faith Cameron was going
to make a success of running the hotel. The owner, Willis
Pinkney, had offered her the job of running it as soon as
he heard that Marge had lit out with Smitty. There was little
likelihood that Marge would return soon, and since Pinkney
had been in partnership with Marge and Smitty, he was now
apparently the sole owner of both the saloon and the hotel.

Pete, by now a favorite with Faith's kids, had accepted
Faith's offer to stay on at the hotel as general handyman,
and was fast making himself indispensable to the widow of
Harley Cameron—in more ways than one, Longarm realized.

"Why potatoes, Longarm?" Matt Stokes asked.

"I'm farm-bred, Matt. And I've seen what can happen
to potatoes in low, wet ground. This high, cool country is
made for the potato. You won't get any rot up here. That
means you can leave the potato in the ground. If you do
that, it'll grow to enormous size."

MacLaggan leaned closer. "I can see that, Longarm. I
guess you're makin' sense after all. Go on."

"You get eight times as many pounds of potatoes as you
do any grain on the same acre of soil. It's the ideal crop
for a small, one-family homestead. Grain has to be harvested
all at once, and you saw what Radley had to go through to
get labor for harvest. Potatoes can be dug out over the whole
season."

"But where the hell are we going to *sell* all those potatoes?" Matt asked.

"There are mining camps springing up all around. I heard
there was a gold strike just north of here. Read about it
when I was passing through Ogden. Hell, you won't have
any trouble selling potatoes. It's a staple. And it don't have
to be milled. Just peeled, cooked, and eaten."

MacLaggan shook his head. "I don't know."

Longarm got to his feet.

"It's just a suggestion," he told them. "That's all. You can grow what you want. It's your farm and your soil. But I warn you, I better not hear that any of you are making moonshine."

"Hell!" said MacLaggan. "After that job you and Matt here did on my still, it'll be a while—even if I did have good enough land to grow barley."

"Or," said Matt Stokes, "the ranch hands to harvest it."

Longarm clapped his hat on and tugged it down snugly.

"I promised myself I'd move out early today," he said. "Thanks for coming in to hear my warning—and my suggestion. Think on it. It won't hurt to do that much. I'll be going in to say goodbye to Faith now, gentlemen."

Faith was at the sink washing her hands when Longarm entered the kitchen. She hurriedly dried them on a towel and turned to face him. Since the day before, she was no longer wearing mourning dress. He was glad to see it.

"Going now?" she asked.

He nodded. "My horse is outside, waiting at the hitch rail."

"Thank you, Longarm. For everything."

"I'm right sorry about Harley, Faith. I wish I could've saved him."

"Don't dwell on it, Longarm," she told him. "Life must go on. I have the children to remind me of him. That will have to do. But I feel terribly sorry for the others. For Bo and for Cal Hardman—and for that poor young girl, Annabelle." She smiled. "Harley loved her, you know. In a sense, he gave his life for her. He was a fine man."

"You knew? About your husband and Annabelle?"

"Yes, of course. A woman knows when someone else shares her husband's embraces, Longarm. I didn't know who it was until she rode in with you. The look in Harley's eyes told me the rest." She glanced out the window. Longarm saw tears coursing down her cheeks. "And now they lie together out there in that lonely valley."

"If it's any comfort," Longarm said, "Annabelle told me how much she admired you—and how ashamed she was."

Faith looked back at Longarm and smiled at him through her tears. "I could tell that too. Annabelle tried so hard to show me how she felt. I was so glad that she never told me outright, though. About Harley, I mean. That would have made it . . . too difficult."

Yes, Longarm thought. That would have, indeed. "Goodbye, Faith," he said.

"Goodbye, Longarm." She stood on her tiptoes and planted a kiss on his cheek. "That's to remember me by," she said.

Longarm grinned. "I'm glad Pete didn't see that. He'd likely come after me with a meat cleaver."

Faith blushed.

About fifty miles south of Red Gap three days later, Longarm made camp by an icy, very swift stream and built a campfire. He put a lot of attention to it, ranging far to get the dry twigs and kindling he needed. Soon, as dusk fell, he had a fine, leaping fire that closely resembled a Fourth of July bonfire, at least as far as enthusiasm was concerned.

But this wasn't July, and Longarm wasn't celebrating any national holidays. He just wanted a beacon of light bright enough to guide those two riders he had glimpsed on a ridge behind him late yesterday afternoon and early this morning. They were the same riders in each case, though he had been unable—at that distance—to make out who they were. With this blazing campfire he was hoping he would be able to coax them out of the cool night.

Alongside the roaring fire he built a dummy of himself out of rocks and his saddle, the entire effigy covered by his horse blanket. Then he moved up into the rocks above the camp and waited.

The moon had turned into a silver dollar almost directly overhead, blotting out all but the brightest stars, when Longarm saw someone moving through the shadows toward his camp. Cautiously he picked up his rifle as the intruder moved into the ring of light cast by the still-glowing embers of his campfire. The dim figure glanced quickly around, like a wild beast that has sensed danger. It was that quick, feline glance that told Longarm who it was.

Marge Pennock.

She did not look good. Her hair was a rat's nest; her

178

dress was filthy, and where it was not soiled, it was ripped. "Longarm," she cried softly, hurrying to Longarm's stony double curled up near the campfire. "Longarm! Wake up!"

She bent over and reached down to shake Longarm awake. He heard her startled scream as she jumped back, and stood up from his concealment.

Longarm stood up.

"Hold it right there, Marge," he said, calling down to her. "Where's your partner? And remember, I've got a loaded rifle in my hand."

"He's right behind you," growled Smitty.

Longarm started to turn, but got only halfway as Smitty's powerful fist struck him in the side of the head and sent him tumbling down the rocky slope. Twisting head over heels, he struck hard and lay at the foot of the slope, dazed. With a squeal of terror, Marge glanced up the slope at Smitty.

"I knew where I'd find you, bitch!" he cried, scrambling down the slope and snatching up Longarm's rifle.

Marge turned to run. Smitty fired. The bullet struck her in the back and sent her sprawling forward—into the campfire. At once the flames exploded back to their earlier vitality as the embers lit her dress—and a moment later her hair. Thrashing wildly, Marge screamed and tried to roll out of the fire. But she was too badly wounded.

She could only lie there and burn.

Longarm flung himself at Smitty. But the big man was waiting for him. Swinging the rifle like a club, he caught Longarm in the midsection with the stock. Longarm went down heavily, gasping, his senses reeling as he fought down the urge to retch.

His vision swimming painfully, he saw Smitty lever a fresh cartridge into the Winchester's firing chamber and aim the rifle at him. There was a sharp crack—and Smitty sagged to his knees. When he tried to raise the rifle again, another gunshot sounded. This time the round caught Smitty in the side of his neck, knocking him to the ground.

Still hugging his gut, Longarm moved swiftly past the dying man and pulled Marge from the fire. He beat out the flames with his bare hands, then rolled her over. He wished he hadn't. Her blistered face was puckered like that of a woman of ninety. Her eyes resembled charred coals. A hole in her face just below what was left of her nose moved, and a sibilant parody of her voice whispered, "Is that you, Longarm?"

"It's me."

Longarm heard footsteps behind him, and glanced up. Sits Tall Woman and Black Elk, carrying the Henry rifle that had belonged to Doc Ramsdell, were approaching.

Longarm looked back down at Marge. "Stay quiet, Marge. We'll get you to a doctor."

"No . . . Let me die . . . Deserve it . . . Want you to know. Smitty . . . made me go with him. Didn't want to."

"Shh," he told her. "Lie quiet. You don't have to tell me any more."

"No. Must tell." A blackened hand reached up. He took it in his own. "When I got a chance . . . took his horse and left him. He was wounded bad . . . thought he wouldn't catch me. Then you and me . . . with all that gold. But the horses bolted. Smitty caught me . . ."

She stopped and her tongue tried to moisten her baked lips. Her hand squeezed his. "Saw . . . you. Tried to catch up. Couldn't . . ."

"Don't try to speak," he told her. "Just rest."

She shook her head, then tried to tell him more, but all she could manage was a faint, barely perceptible rasping sound—like that of dry leaves moving before a cold wind.

Longarm stood up and let her die.

It was the following night, and Black Elk was gone. He had accepted Smitty's saddlebag, heavy with gold coins, which Longarm had given him, and was on his way back to Red Gap with it. There, in accordance with Longarm's instructions, he would divide the gold evenly between those families who had suffered from Radley's depredations. Longarm thought he knew what Faith Cameron would do with her cut—purchase an equal share in the hotel.

He had an idea where Rosita Sanchez had gotten all that gold. Her father. His career as a highwayman, it seemed, had not been entirely unlucky. Longarm realized that perhaps he should have brought the gold back with him and made an honest attempt to locate its rightful owners; but he had decided instead that it was time now for the gold to bring good fortune rather than bad, life rather than death.

Sits Tall Woman threw a few more branches on the fire, then returned to their blanket. She had insisted on going with him at least as far as Taylor's Ferry, and Longarm had found no reason to discourage her.

As she snuggled her nakedness close against his, she smiled up at him. Her dark, almond-shaped eyes gleamed with passion. Her body he had found as supple as a sapling and as smooth as imported silk. Her breasts against his nakedness were globes of warmth that thrilled him clear through. Smiling down at her, he cradled her head in the crook of his arm and kissed her on the lips.

"Mmm," she said, when he had finished the kiss and was nibbling softly on her earlobe. "Longarm kiss gentle. Soon he will have much fire, maybe?"

"Shhh," he said softly, his finger tracing the contour of one of her breasts. "No more talking."

She laughed. "Fools Crow was right," she whispered. "He say if you not need our help, you might like my comfort."

Longarm smiled, then covered her lips with his own. It had been Black Elk and Sits Tall Woman that Longarm had seen following him. Frank Fools Crow had discovered that he had not lost his powers after all, and had had a vision that warned him of bad trouble stalking Longarm. Still too weak to ride himself, Fools Crow had sent his brother and sister instead.

It was clear that Longarm owed his life to Frank Fools Crow's prescient powers. He figured it would be foolhardy, therefore, to ignore any other of the medicine man's suggestions.

He enclosed Sits Tall Woman in his arms and pulled her still closer to him. Her soft laughter warmed him. She thrust herself still closer against him and he felt, building within him, all the fire that Sits Tall Woman could handle—and perhaps just a little bit more.

Watch for

LONGARM IN YUMA

**forty-third novel in the
LONGARM series from Jove**

coming in April

LONGARM

LONGARM